A suburban dream turns into a nightmare...

Beau had moved to Isabelle's side and was sitting next to her, gazing alertly at Peter. The minute Peter rose from his chair and took a step forward, wanting somehow to apologize, to touch her hair and say he was sorry, Beau interposed himself between them, and a low growl rumbled in his throat. Another step forward, and his lip curled back, revealing his teeth.

For the first time Peter was afraid of him....

UNABLE TO FIND FAWCETT PAPERBACKS AT
YOUR LOCAL BOOKSTORE OR NEWSSTAND?

If you are unable to locate a book published by Fawcett, or, if you wish to see a list of all available Fawcett Crest, Gold Medal and Popular Library titles, write for our FREE Order Form. Just send us your name and address and 35¢ to help defray postage and handling costs. Mail to:

FAWCETT BOOKS GROUP
P.O. Box C730
524 Myrtle Ave.
Pratt Station, Brooklyn, N.Y. 11205

(Orders for less than 5 books must include 75¢ for the first book and 25¢ for each additional book to cover postage and handling.)

BEST FRIEND

a novel by
Pat Feeley

FAWCETT CREST • NEW YORK

To Tom and Michael and Hy, for their confidence, encouragement, and sound advice, and many kindnesses; and to the animals I have known and loved, especially to Serena and Stokely Catmichael and to Sarge, who gave up countless hours of canine pleasure to snooze at my feet as I wrote.

BEST FRIEND

THIS BOOK CONTAINS THE COMPLETE TEXT OF THE ORIGINAL HARDCOVER EDITION.

Published by Fawcett Crest Books, a unit of CBS Publications, the Consumer Publishing Division of CBS Inc., by arrangement with Elsevier-Dutton Publishing Company, Inc.

Copyright © 1977 by Patricia Falk Feeley

ALL RIGHTS RESERVED

All the characters in this book are fictitious, and any resemblance to actual persons living or dead is purely coincidental.

Printed in the United States of America

10 9 8 7 6 5 4 3 2 1

Even long afterward, Roger Stanley had times when he would awaken in panic, his heart hammering in his chest, his body soaked in sweat. He could never remember the details of his nightmare. He did not want to.

1

The fire that Peter Buckingham had set an hour before, and that he was poking so nervously at the moment, blazed up the old stone chimney, and flickered warmly across the paneled walls of his study. In ordinary circumstances, it would certainly have dispelled the gloom of a howling March night that sent sleet rattling against the windows. But the circumstances, on this particular evening, were not ordinary.

Peter left off making himself so fruitlessly busy, hung the poker back on its hook, and slumped into his worn leather wing chair. He closed his eyes for a moment and rubbed his jaw with his knuckles. Then he drew himself up again and turned once more to his wife, Isabelle. She was crouched anxiously on a flowered rug by his feet, stroking their elderly springer spaniel, Patchwork. The old dog's once glossy brown and white coat shone dull and dry in the reflected firelight. His breathing was rough, his sleep fitful. Clearly, he was nearing the end.

Peter's thoughts turned back to the time, fifteen long years ago, when he'd brought Patchwork home. John had been only fourteen then, Anne barely ten. Patch had been very much their puppy at first, a round, bouncey ball always trying to keep up with the kids. Later, when Patch had grown up and settled down a bit, Peter had patiently trained him to hunt. For eight seasons, before Patch had begun to slow down, man and dog had spent weekends trudging the woods and fields and duck marshes, providing the game for countless little dinners.

The old fellow had truly been a family pet, but his care had always fallen to Isabelle, and Peter knew it was to Isabelle that Patch had always been most devoted. The last few years he had become, increasingly, a focus for Isabelle's life. With her children gone—off to college and into lives of their own—and with her husband traveling more frequently and for longer periods on business, she had made Patch her full-time companion. He made her feel needed, in a way no one else did any more. He filled her days with love, with presence, with dependence.

It was she, after all, who fed him, brushed him every day, gave him his medicine, took him everywhere, reciprocated his devotion. It was she who would, now that he was dying, miss him the most. That was what was worrying Peter. Now it was no longer possible that Patch would get better, that his stiffness would ease, that the disturbing extra sound his heart made as it pumped would go away. Peter had arrived home, an hour before, from a trip to Houston, to find Isabelle sitting with the old dog in the near dark, stroking him quietly, with the tears running down her face. Peter had telephoned Roger Stanley, who was not just their vet but an old friend as well, and asked him to come right away. He'd thought that there might be something that Roger could do or say, something that he himself could not find in his repertoire of soothing words. Christ, he felt like crying himself, not just for old Patch, but for the passage of the fifteen years between the day they'd brought him home and this wintry night.

Waiting for Roger, they'd passed an hour already, Isabelle never moving from the old dog's side, Peter trying to distract her with cheerful, if forced, reminiscences of Patch's long lifetime. As a puppy, his fondness for dragging every shoe and sock in the house into a pile to be admired by his family. His career as a mighty hunter, arriving home triumphantly with a coat full of burrs and a self-satisfied expression. But Peter had run out of material for what was, in essence, a monologue, and began to wonder where in hell Roger was, and whether there was anything that could really cheer Isabelle up.

Isabelle had always been shy, painfully so, and it had been that shyness, along with her seeming eagerness to please, that had first attracted Peter to her all those summers ago. "Dizzy," he'd called her then, teasingly, since she'd been anything but. He could close his eyes and see her as she was then, pretty and pale and fragile-looking, but with a streak of determination that he liked. She'd been working as a secretary in a law office, back when you could still read law for the bar exam. Funny, he hadn't thought of that in years. Her father, a stern and old-fashioned lawyer himself, had considered law not a profession for women and had refused to let her attend law school. A hard man, his father-in-law. Very hard. But fair, and probably right. The whole thing had simply dropped within days of the time Peter had met Isabelle. They had fallen in love, danced and dreamed, and married. When the children had come, they'd moved to Darien, and Peter had been pleased to find that Isabelle had unexpected gifts as a mother, a housekeeper, a complete wife. He admired her gift for gardening, which occupied her spring and summer, and for needlework, with which she passed long evenings. Just what a wife should be.

But she made few friends. Madeleine Stanley, Roger's wife, dead these five years, had been the only one he could think of. Maybe it wasn't so easy to make friends in a town like this, a Connecticut commuter town, a place where a quarter of the homes changed hands every year. You'd meet a congenial couple, and just as you were getting to know them, a transfer would come along and they'd be gone. What did it matter to the men? Wherever they went, they had their work, but it could be rough on the women. In time, he'd come to realize that Isabelle's shyness was something of a handicap. Not that he wanted her to be pushy. He hated pushy women. But that he wanted her to fit in better to ease the burden on him. On the few trips she'd taken with him, however pleasant and polite she'd been, she just hadn't fit in, and he'd felt as though she should. So Isabelle had begun to decline his invitations to join him, and he'd stopped asking. Now he went alone—though he didn't always travel like a hermit. There wasn't a city in the country where a reasonably attractive out-of-towner couldn't meet a reasonably attractive woman and enjoy with her anything from a couple of drinks to a brief affair.

The arrangement was what it was. She confined herself to home, to the things that suited her, to what she found comfortable, taking care never to question him and always to make his homecoming the most pleasant of rituals. Maybe the ritual didn't signify much anymore, except continuing good will, but it went on, in its comforting way, and he supposed it always would. He wouldn't have considered asking Isabelle what she thought of it, but he was, as he glanced back at her again, moved by the thirty years of her fidelity and goodness, moved that he could still see in the woman the girl he'd loved so long ago. He reached out and touched her hair, still soft and blonde, though streaked with gray.

From outside, Peter heard the unmistakable roar of Roger's unmuffled Land Rover.

"Must be him," he said, starting for the door. But before he could reach it, Roger threw it open himself and stamped into the little slate entry hall, water dripping from his Army-issue poncho and boots, from his grizzled sandy hair and mustache, from his ruddy weather-worn face, and from his small leather doctor's bag. He shook himself, for all the world like one of his own canine patients, so that even Isabelle, upset as she was, peered around the door into the hall, laughing, and called to him, "Lord, Rog. Don't worry about the water. Just get out of your wet things and come in by the fire."

Peter, rummaging through the hall closet, emerged with a boot jack and, helping his friend out of his soggy clothing, told him quietly what he'd found when he got home. Roger responded in a fashion that could only have come from thirty years of suburban practice, his tone avuncular, his manner calm. "There now, Pete. There might be something we can do, but there might not. It's natural that Izzy's upset. But she's a grown girl, and she knows that no pet lives forever. That's the hard part. Let's see what we can do."

With that, he gave himself a final shake, picked up his bag, and marched into the study. Bending down, he gave Isabelle a hearty hug and a kiss on the cheek. "There, darling Iz," he said, "I know it's awful, but be a good girl and get the lights on so I can see what we can do for the old fellow." As she rose, he took her place on the rug beside Patch, and opened his bag. By this time, the dog was awake, trying to lift his head and to wag a greeting for his old friend. Rog, talking softly to him, ran his large square hands gently but firmly from shoulder to tail, down the ribs and along the back. He shook his head, and pulled the stethoscope from the bag, fitting the earpieces carefully, and moving the instrument slowly, carefully, ever so gently, from place to place along Patch's heaving sides.

Finally, he sat back, removed the stethoscope, and put it back in the bag. He straightened his shoulders, and looked up at Isabelle for a long, silent moment. When he spoke, his voice was clear and firm. "Isabelle, I'm not going to tell you what to do, but I'm going to tell you what's the matter and what I think you *should* do. Patch has heart trouble. You know that. Now the lungs are congested, and the heart is failing. There's nothing that I can or should do with a dog this age, in this condition, to correct the problem. It would cause him pain, when he's not in pain right now—uncomfortable, sure, but not in pain. This thing is going to get worse, and he's going to die. My best advice is that we let him go. I have the overdose in my bag. I can give it to him right now, and it won't hurt at all. That way he can go right here, right in front of his own fire, with his pals around him. What do you say?"

She turned to Peter, looking for help, but all he could do was to shrug and say, "Up to you, dear." All her distress and bewilderment sounded in her voice, strangled by tears. She shook her head to clear it. "I knew, Rog, of course I did. And I know you're right. It's just hard, that's all. But it's harder on him, I guess...."

"Come on, Iz, I need your permission," Rog said, his voice soothing, coaxing. She nodded in confirmation.

"Now," said Rog, commandingly, "you go in the kitchen and get us each a good stiff drink, so we'll have something to toast the old fellow in. And you, Pete, you bring me down a comforter or something." He fondled the dog's ears, giving Peter and Isabelle time to leave the room, and then pulled from his bag a disposable syringe and a vial of clear liquid. He filled the syringe, carefully and completely, pushed a drop or two of shining liquid from the tip of the needle, grasped the animal's right paw in his left hand, and inserted the needle cleanly in the vein. "There you go, Patch," he said as he finished and tossed the syringe back in his bag, "it won't be long now." By the time the Buckinghams came back, Rog had resumed his reassuring stroking of the dog, who saluted them with one last flicker of his tail before he fell asleep.

Rog sat in Isabelle's chair, Peter in his own, she on the floor with Patch, her hand resting lightly on his ribs. She wanted, for some reason, to mark the exact second when his breathing stopped, but Rog launched into a story about some bygone hunting trip, the one on which Patch had had his first encounter with a floating duck blind and had tipped the whole affair and both men into the water on a chill November morning. It was an old story, a family favorite that had been told many times, but it never did seem to dim. Distracted for a moment, she joined in the laughter, warm with the memory of good times. By the time the laughter subsided the raspy sound of Patch's breathing had turned to silence.

"Rog," she said. "Rog. Is that it?"

"Yes, Iz, I think so."

He got on his knees and pulled the stethoscope out to listen again.

"Yes. It's over."

"Now what?" she said, her voice catching again.

Rog patted her hand awkwardly. "Now, Iz, I'm going to let the old fellow finish his last long sleep by the fire, while I finish my drink. And then I'll wrap him in the quilt and take him back to the hospital. I'd guess you'll want him cremated, so you can sprinkle his ashes down by the Sound later on. Right?"

"I guess so, Rog. When you put it that way. I know dogs don't live forever, and I know maybe I'm silly. But, yes. Please do that for me, won't you?"

She took a sip of her drink and turned to Peter. "That's okay, Peter, isn't it?"

"Yes, of course. Just fine. Just right." Privately, he thought it was a little strange, but he wasn't going to say so, or upset her any more, or risk some scene that would go out of his control. Apparently Rog thought it was the right thing to do, and he surely knew about these things.

Rog broke the pause by asking Isabelle to pour him another drink. When she'd left the room, he turned to Peter.

"Pete, I know it may seem funny to you, but I think Iz is going to have one hell of a time with Patch gone. That's one of the reasons I came up and did it this way. She's alone a lot, and I think we should talk her into getting another dog. It's the only thing to do. Okay if I raise it now?"

"Jesus, Rog. I don't know. I don't think it can hurt, but I don't want to bring it up. You go ahead."

When she returned with the drinks, Rog pulled her down to perch on the arm of his chair, and put his arm around her. "Iz, I know you feel like hell, and over the next few days you're going to feel a whole lot worse, but I'd like you to help me with something. One of my patients is a grand Belgian shepherd bitch, big sweet-tempered old girl with obedience degrees in the pedigree all the way back. She's just had a fine litter, purebred. They're five weeks, now, and they'll be ready to go in a matter of weeks. I can't think of any way to replace Patchwork, but you ought to have another dog, and soon, too. You're terrific with them, you know. So I'll take you out to see them tomorrow around two if you'll consider it. How about it?"

Isabelle did not want to have a look. But as she had deferred first to her father, then to Peter, she felt it necessary now to defer to Rog. She would go, she thought, and look. But she would not have another dog, would not go through this again. She wanted to be thirty-eight once more, with two lively children, and plenty to do, and a puppy under her feet, but if she could not have that, she did not want substitutes. She could do without. She would make a show—and only a show—of giving in.

"Yes, Rog. I suppose you're right. I don't much feel like it, but it can't hurt to look."

"That's my girl," said Rog. And Peter patted her approvingly. The men were pleased. She would go, look, decline. Simple.

Roger tossed back the rest of his drink, put down the glass, and knelt to wrap Patch carefully in the comforter. She could not watch, and turned away until he had finished and was standing with the sad bundle at his feet. "I'll get my things, Iz, and take him out to the car. And I'll pick you up tomorrow at two, if that's okay with you."

She nodded. "Thanks, Rog. For everything. You're a good friend and a great help."

She walked to the hall with him, Peter trailing behind with the bundle, and helped him on with his coat and boots. The men steered their way to the car, and then Peter came back in, shivering, to put his arm around her and to wave Rog goodbye through the storm door. When the car was out of sight, he turned to her. "Look," he said, "we're both beat, and we both need something to eat. What do you say we go up to the steak house and have something for supper?"

"When?" she said, forgetting. "I haven't fed Patch yet." And burst into tears, sobbing over and over again. "He was all I had anymore. He was all I had." She would not be comforted, and Peter was appalled.

2

Later, when Isabelle had calmed herself, they sat in front of the fire, picking at soup and sandwiches, and trying to make conversation. At last, Isabelle pleaded exhaustion and dragged herself upstairs. Peter tossed another log on the fire, noting as he did so that the sleet had stopped but that the wind had picked up and begun to shrill. He poured himself a brandy and pulled his chair close to the fender, kicking his shoes off and propping his feet on its upholstered rail, letting himself relax for what seemed like the first time in days.

Jesus. Thirty years of marriage, fifty-five years old, two kids raised, and one day the dog dies and your wife tells you that's all she had anymore. Terrific. Where does it end? He closed his eyes for a moment, trying to think, trying to push the fatigue back and think. Maybe a few minutes in the fresh air would help.

Heaving himself out of the chair, he walked over to the window and pulled back the curtains so that he could see his reflection in the glass, not clearly but well enough. He'd never been handsome, but he'd kept his hair, now silvering, and he'd aged pretty well, he thought, his waistline still neat and trim with all the tennis. He always carried a tennis bag with him wherever he went, played every chance he got, had played since he was seven. Boston Latin, Harvard, whenever he could, except during the war, when there'd been no chances.

There'd been no money in it when he was a kid. These days, he would have gone pro, still thought of what it would have been like, when he watched Laver and Ashe and Connors. Especially Connors, he was the one. In him, Peter could see his own stocky build, the scramble on the court, the pugnacious quality that in him had condensed into toughness, aggressiveness, the ability to win over people who should have beaten him. Two years before, and it still thrilled him to think about it, he'd beaten Gardner Mulloy in a pickup match one weekend in Tucson. A great moment. A triumph. Undoubtedly the best moment of his whole life.

Afterwards, in the bar, he'd just felt so good, so friendly, so expansive, even witty. He felt young again, dammit, not the gray chemical company executive from New York, but light and easy, like a young and cocky pro. There'd been a pretty girl in the bar that afternoon, not a girl, but a young woman. He'd had a drink with her, and dinner, and gone back to her room. Her name was Jill, and she was from Los Angeles, and she had long black hair that fell to her hips when she removed from it the single old-fashioned hairpin that held it all in place. Beautiful hair, beautiful and young and somehow magical as it came tumbling down. Again he felt what he'd felt that afternoon, lightness and youth and the disappearance of age. For one evening, he'd loved that girl, loved what the game gave him and what she gave him. He had taken nothing from Isabelle, had just given himself something, had given himself a perfect day.

But, my God, over a dog? Was that really all Isabelle thought she had anymore?

He dropped the curtains, went to the closet, pulled on his ski jacket and shuffled back into his shoes. Then he slipped outside into the cold and dark. He walked around the house, to the side overlooking Long Island Sound, past Isabelle's orderly perennial beds, and down to the wall where, later, summer flowers would be massed against a tangle of species roses. Beyond was the water, and across the water, now that the night was clear, he could see first the lights of Shippan Point and beyond the lights of Long Island's north shore.

Wasn't this something? A fine house and garden, lovingly and even lavishly restored and tended, full of good comfortable things, secure. A son practicing law with a fine old firm. A daughter starting out with an urban planning firm in Chicago. A husband who loved and provided for her. No, he wasn't there as much as he had been, but maybe, soon, he could cut down, leave some of the travel to younger men. He'd make an effort. He was the sort of man who knew that making an effort led, more often than not, to results, and it would work out this time as it always had. Rather like practicing a backhand, it seemed. His right arm swept across his chest in the familiar gesture, that smooth chop that had caught so many opponents off guard. He whipped the invisible ball back toward the invisible opponent, but just outside his reach.

Upstairs, Isabelle had heard him slip out. She hadn't been sleeping, only lying quietly in her half of the big old fourposter that they'd dragged gleefully away from a fashionable Manhattan streetcorner the year they were married. What had been trash to someone else had been treasure to them, and they'd had it ever since. They'd been in love, she remembered, newly married, she—at twenty-three—just pregnant with John. The two of them had dragged it home in a taxi, two trips and after midnight, the driver joining them in laughter, even helping them with it as they dragged it up the stairs, and staying for a brandy against the cold. They had refinished it, repaired it, and—finally finished—had celebrated as though it were something precious bought at great price from Parke Bernet. They'd moved it to Darien with them, to this house, years before, when Anne was a baby. But now, thought Isabelle, she seemed to have it to herself most of the time. No Peter, many nights. He was gone too much. Neither children to creep in in the mornings, nor teenagers to give her all the details of an evening out. Now, even Patch was gone from his accustomed place beside the bed.

She realized that it had been a matter of minutes since she'd heard Peter go out. Curious. She rose and walked lightly to the window, just in time to see him, down by the wall, make that strange backhand swing into the dark. She crept lightly back to bed, and kept her eyes open, listening for him. Soon the hall door clicked open and then shut; then she heard his footsteps and the rattle of hangers as he hung his jacket back in the closet; and after that the sounds of locks being checked and lights doused for the night. Finally she heard him on the stairs, for, softly as he walked, the stairs themselves—steep and old and slightly out of true—creaked with every shift of weight. For years, when the children were young, she'd worried about those stairs, but they didn't bother her now, she thought wryly, and wouldn't until it was a question of her own balance. Peter, thinking her asleep, eased the door open.

"It's okay, Peter. I'm still awake. Come on to bed."

He sat down on the edge of the bed, and she reached for his hand. "I know you must be tired, dear. This on top of your trip. Maybe you can sleep a little later in the morning, but it must be nearly midnight."

He drew his hand away and rubbed his eyes. "I just can't seem to unwind, Isabelle. Maybe I should fix myself some cocoa or something, and watch television for a while. I'm tired, but I don't think I can sleep. And you must be whipped."

"Yes, I really am. But I wouldn't mind some company and a snuggle. It's been a lousy day."

"Okay. Look, I'm going to change into my pajamas and robe, and get some cocoa, and then I'll come back up. Want some?"

"No, you go ahead. Are you going to stay downstairs, or bring it back up here?"

"I guess I'll watch Johnny Carson, and drink the stuff, and come up when I feel more relaxed, okay?"

"Anything that suits you, dear, but I'm not sure I can stay awake."

He bent down, and brushed her hair with his lips. "See you in a little while, then."

But he didn't come upstairs until nearly one o'clock, and by then she was sound asleep.

3

The next morning, Isabelle rose at six-thirty, quietly slipping into her bathrobe and scuffs and tiptoeing out the bedroom door. She knew that Peter would not want to be disturbed so early. The day after he came back from one of his trips, he liked to sleep late, to catch the 8:57 train from Darien rather than his more usual 8:13, to enjoy a certain contrived sense of leisure that let him take it just a bit easier than usual. And she had no idea when he'd finally gotten to bed.

Besides, she had something she wanted to do this morning before he came down, something that would clearly confirm her decision not to have another dog, something that would remove from her sight all the visible reminders of Patch and thus of his permanent and irrevocable absence.

When she reached the bottom of the stairs, she picked up the plaid cushion that had for so long occupied the downstairs landing and provided him his daytime retreat. She slipped his leash from the rack in the hall, and carried both things into the kitchen, where she went through the cupboards for several remaining cans of dog food, a half-empty carton of biscuits, and a sack of kibble. All these things she stuffed into a couple of brown paper bags. His dishes went the same way, and the leash, souvenir of all the miles he'd walked with her, went last. Shrugging into a sheepskin coat against the morning chill, she carried the bed and the sacks out to the garbage cans in the garage, stuffed everything tightly down, and returned to the kitchen.

When Peter came down at seven-thirty, she was sitting at the kitchen table with a cup of coffee. "My, you're the early bird this morning," he said, bending to kiss the air near her left ear. "What have you been up to?"

"Getting rid of Patch's things," she said.

"Why? What if you get another dog? You'll be able to use some of them at least. It seems kind of silly, Isabelle."

Her tone was edgy, not angry but close to it. "Look, those things were his. If we get another dog, I think we can afford to get him his own things. That's first of all. Second, I agreed to look at those puppies today, but I don't think I want one. I miss Patch, and I know I'm bound to miss him more, but who could go through this again? I'd feel disloyal anyway, wouldn't you?"

"On the contrary. When you've been happy enough with one to want another, that's kind of a tribute to the first one, I'd guess."

She stared thoughtfully out the window for a moment, tracing the edge of her saucer with one finger. "And there's another thing, too, Peter. We've got this big place, and it was a grand family house for years and years, but it's too big for us now, really. If we didn't have the responsibility of a house, not even the responsibility of an animal, we could do more things together, you know? We could move into town, get some place we could just lock the door on, travel a little, go to the theater. I'd enjoy it, and so would you. And you wouldn't have to commute anymore. We loved it in the city when we first got married. Think of all the things we did together then, when we were first starting out. Do you remember?"

As she spoke, the disapproval that she could read in that first tightening of the jaw muscles turned slowly into a stern, almost bullying expression, and his face began to flush. Suddenly, he slammed his hand against the table hard enough to make the coffee cups dance.

"Move out of here? After all we've put into

this? You must be kidding. And into some rented, overpriced box in town? Christ, what an idea! And for what? The odd night at the theater? The dubious pleasure of being mugged on the way home? The fun of paying twenty dollars an hour for a tennis court? Everything we want is out here. Fresh air, a lovely home, recreation, shopping, everything. If we want to, we can lock the door on this place, you know. If we want to go somewhere, we can put the dog in a kennel. Even if I were commuting five days a week, which I seldom am, I'd rather live here, and you would, too. I love it out here—always have, always have that feeling when I get on the train that I've made it out, by God. I'm on that train to Connecticut, to my beautiful house and my lovely wife, and I've made it out. I won't even consider moving back."

He stopped abruptly, and swirled his coffee impatiently in his cup, regaining his composure. "Now, Isabelle, for God's sake be reasonable. Rog is right. You *are* alone a lot, and a dog is good company and good protection for you. I think you need it. You wouldn't want another springer, I know, or even a spaniel, but these shepherds are different from that. You go look and decide. I'd better get going, or I'm going to miss that train."

"Peter," she said, her voice under tight control, "I just don't want one right now. Period. It's too soon, all right?"

"It really is entirely up to you. I only want what's right for you. If you don't want it, fine, but go take a look."

Her answer was so quiet that he could barely hear it. "Please don't be patronizing. I can take a lot of things, but I can't take that. I promised Rog I'd go, and I will."

He reached for her hand. "I didn't mean it that way," he said. "Look, let's go out to dinner tonight, all right? You be ready when I get home. How about that?"

Within a few minutes, Peter had wheeled his silver Porsche out of the driveway toward the station, and she dawdled over her second cup of coffee, the hours until two o'clock yawning before her. She thought that she could get through them by keeping busy. First she could shower and dress, then put the kitchen and the study and the bedroom and bath in order. The rest of the house they hardly used anymore, but maybe she could clean a closet or something. It was too cold to garden for long, but she could begin to work on the scraggly raspberry canes at the side of the house. She could call the kids and tell them about Patch. And she could do Peter's laundry from his trip and take some of his things to the cleaner's. That could occupy her until noon or so.

She shivered, feeling more alone in the house than she ever had. She glanced at the place where Patch's dishes had always sat. It seemed stripped rather than merely vacant.

She had to get moving, she knew that, so she got up and put her dishes in the dishwasher and dragged herself upstairs to shower.

Afterward she dressed quickly in warm pants, a turtleneck, wool socks, and topsiders. In minutes, she had completed the little straightening up that the house needed, and tossed Peter's clothes in the washer. She watched it fill, her eye caught by the graceful curve of the water flowing into the machine, thinking of the days when the children lived at home and of the work, real work, that housework had entailed then. She'd complained about it, of course, like any mother, had nagged at them to pick up after themselves. But she'd enjoyed, all the same, the feeling of accomplishment she'd had when she finished the work in time, just in time, to relax for a half hour before John and Anne had come tumbling home from school with Patch barking at their heels. She laughed at herself for missing the noise and the clutter and the confusion.

What had it been like lately? She'd do her morning chores and then, in any weather that could be considered even passable, she'd put Patch on his leash and walk him down to the beach. That walk had slowed down a lot as he aged. They'd always be gone for at least an hour and lately it had often been closer to two. He'd hunt in the bushes along the way, play on the beach when they got there, retrieve hunks of seaweed for her. And she'd sit on the breakwater or on the porch of the lifeguard's cottage, and read or do her needlework or talk to a strange and wonderful old man who seemed to appear, on his bicycle, from nowhere at all. He seemed a little crazy, but he was friendly and kind and good-humored. His clothes were worn but spotlessly clean, and their pockets were always stuffed with dog biscuits in all three sizes. He didn't own a dog himself, but he was obviously fond of them, carefully selecting the proper-sized bone for each of his numerous four-footed friends. No one knew his name, it seemed. She simply thought of him as The Old Man.

She should walk down to the beach. He'd be there today, and she'd tell him about Patch. The problem was that she couldn't, somehow, walk down there without a dog. The dog had been the reason, or at least the excuse, for these excursions.

She dumped the detergent in and slammed the top of the washer shut. She could hardly stand there until two o'clock. What to do? She'd call the children. They'd want to know.

She put it off for a few minutes longer by pouring herself another cup of coffee and rummaging the drawers for a cigarette. Peter had given it up years before, but she never could, and was an occasional secret smoker. This morning she needed it. She took her cup, cigarettes, and ashtray in to the desk in the study, and dialed Anne's number in Chicago.

There was clicking on the line, and then the

switchboard operator's voice, and some more clicking, and a secretary's voice, and then, finally, Anne. "Mother, what's the matter?"

"I'm sorry, dear. I didn't mean to scare you. Dad's fine, and so am I, but I thought I ought to let you know that Patch is gone."

"God, you really frightened me. They called me out of a meeting. I'm really sorry, Mother, but I'm glad you're all right. How'd it happen?"

"Well, you know he's been failing, and finally his heart just wasn't working. Rog came over last night and put him down, right here. At least he didn't suffer."

"Well, that's something, anyway. Is Dad home?"

"Yes. He and Rog are already trying to push me into getting another dog. One of Rog's patients had some puppies, and he's dragging me up there to see them this afternoon. To tell you the truth, though, Anne, I'd rather not. We've lived out here for years, but this place is too big for us. I'd rather get an apartment and do more things with your father—you know, something we could just lock the door on, that wouldn't take so much looking after. I might even go back to work, especially if we moved into town."

Anne laughed. "Go back to work, Mother? At your age? Not really. And you wouldn't be happy back in the city. Neither would Dad. Look, get this dog, or some other dog. You need the company. You really should get out more, anyway, and make some new friends."

Isabelle took a long drag on her cigarette, and exhaled slowly before she spoke, trusted herself to speak, without sounding as resentful as she felt. "Okay, Anne. Okay. I just thought you'd want to know, that's all. You go on back to your meeting, and I'll give you a call over the weekend and let you know what happened."

"Okay. Fine. Talk to you then. Give Dad a hug for me."

Isabelle hung the receiver back in its cradle, sipped at her lukewarm coffee. She hated Peter, absolutely hated him, when he was as peremptory and patronizing as he'd been this morning. And Anne was no better. *"At your age."* *What a thing to say.* And what was the matter with her age? Fifty-three was not exactly one foot in the grave, after all. They always knew best, or thought they did. *Damn!* Maybe Johnny would understand how she felt. He'd always been the one that really seemed to care about her, to have some connection with her. She felt the tears begin to well up again, and lit another cigarette to scorch away the lump in her throat. In a few minutes, she was calm enough to dial his number. In almost no time, the switchboard operator had put her through to him.

"Johnny, it's Mother."

"Hi, there. What a pleasure. Hope nothing's wrong."

"Not that wrong, dear, but Rog had to come and put Patch down last night."

"Oh, Jesus, I'm really sorry. He was a grand old dog, and I know you're going to miss him."

"I already do. The house is absolutely empty without him. I can't even seem to take my walk to the beach. And Dad and Rog and Annie are all after me to get another dog right away—bullying, really."

"Look, Mom, I know how that can be, and I know how you feel. But don't say no just because they're leaning on you. Make up your own mind. Promise?"

"Well," she said, her voice shaking a bit, "I'd like *something*, you know. It's awful to be all alone. And losing an animal is tougher, in some ways, than losing a person. I mean, when Grandpa died, I was sorry and I was upset. He was my father, and I loved him. But you can't love a person as unequivocally and unambiguously as you do an animal. With people, you have conflict and pain and resentment. That's natural enough. But with an animal...an animal accepts you the way you are. Do you know what I mean? Do I sound crazy? I'm not getting this out very well."

"Look, Mom. I know what you mean and it isn't crazy at all."

"Thanks, dear. Look, I'm going to see these puppies today with Rog, and I'll talk to you later. Maybe you and your girl can come have dinner over the weekend or something."

"Can't this weekend, Mom. Alison and I have been asked out to visit one of her friends—an author, really. We're leaving this afternoon. I'll call you next week, though, and see how it went. Okay?"

Alison, his roommate—what other term was there?—worked for a publisher, seemed formidably intelligent, and seemed to lunch at Lutèce about twice a week. She knew a lot of writers whose work Isabelle never seemed to be able to read.

"Sure. Fine, Johnny. And thanks. You've helped."

"Talk to you soon."

Well, she thought, as she moved Peter's laundry from the washer to the dryer, *John's right. I should make up my own mind, I suppose. But if I do get the dog, those three will crow so, thinking they talked me into it.*

It was still only ten-thirty, so Isabelle carried the things for dry cleaning out to the car, wrote out a short shopping list, shrugged back into her sheepskin, and turned her neat brown Volvo station wagon up the Point, past the Zieglers' impeccable wrought iron fences and the greening meadows dotted with their white Charolais cattle. She reflected once more, as she so often had, on the incongruity of that splendid place, with its great stone main house, the gatekeeper's enormous cottage, the imposing barns and outbuildings and—out of sight—the big private anchorage. Forty miles from New York, an hour's drive, it seemed like something left over from a different time or place. Maybe it belonged, would have belonged, fifty miles from Bordeaux, or in the pages of a Scott Fitzgerald novel, but it struck her, every time she passed it, that it wasn't of the here and now.

But then, Darien was removed in its way, so much greener and more prosperous and well-mannered than most of the suburbs, so nearly devoid of anything that was not white, Christian, and upper class. Dissociated. Quiet. She thought of living in the city again, of being back in a setting that would be vital and diverse, of being able to borrow a new kind of energy from the surroundings. And then she was past the Ziegler place, on the twisting back road into town.

Her errands finished, she picked up a paper and went home. The mail had come—mainly circulars and a stream of charity appeals. As she heated some soup, she plowed into the *Times*, giggling a bit over a nasty restaurant review, checking the movie listings as she ate her lunch. Just as she was rinsing her dishes, Rog roared into the driveway and announced his arrival with a wholly superfluous blast of the horn. Waving to him out the kitchen window, she put her dishes in the sink, grabbed her coat and bag, and hurried out to the car.

"Izzy, girl, how are you this morning?" he asked when she got in. "I hope the world looks better to you than it did last night. Aside from everything else, at least the weather's an improvement." And it was, bright and clear and cold.

"Yes, much better, thanks. I'm sorry I was so upset last night."

"That's all right, dear. Perfectly natural. I see it all the time, and I know it's rough. It's good of you to come and see the pups."

"You didn't tell me where we were going. Who's the owner?"

He flicked the gearshift, and the car shot out of the drive, spraying gravel, and, with a screech of tires, headed north.

"Evvy and Tom Hutchinson. You've met them, haven't you? They live up behind Ox Ridge, which is one of the things that makes this so convenient. I've got a couple of horses to attend to, so I can drop you at Evvy's while I do it. Mike Russell's best polo pony pulled up lame on Sunday, and I've been trying to get him sorted out in time for the Fairfield match. And Nancy Raggazi pushed that hunter of hers too hard again, which was hard enough on Nance, but a lot harder on the horse. I shouldn't be more than an hour, though."

As they crossed the Ring's End Bridge, Isabelle glanced at the back of the car, full of tidy metal cases packed with instruments and supplies, and a couple of cages for transporting small animals.

Turning back to Rog, she said, "You don't play polo any more, do you, Rog?"

"No, I just passed the point at which I could

actually enjoy the prospect of getting broken into little pieces once a season. I'm the team vet, though, so I still go to all the matches. The fun kind of went out of it when Madeleine died, I guess. Remember? You and Pete used to come, too, and you and Maddy would make the picnic in summer, and lay it out on the tailgates."

"I guess we both still miss her, Rog. You must, and I know I do."

"It's not as bad as it was, but I can still see her sitting at the dining room table the night she told me. She just announced that she was dying, that she was sorry to be leaving, and that she'd do the best she could with it. She did, too—brave and graceful to the end. But I doubt if I'll ever forgive her for not being here. That's what surprises you afterward—the rage."

Roger zigged left through the stoplight at Ring's End and the Post Road, and zagged right onto Noroton Avenue, with a merry wave at one of the patrol cars parked next to the Presbyterian church. The Land Rover, Isabelle guessed, had become a matter of rueful contemplation for the local police, who'd cited Roger for the lack of a muffler so often they'd apparently given up on him. The officer in the patrol car, in any case, simply waved back.

"Anger is always a surprise, isn't it, Rog? I get angry at Peter now, and I almost never did, before. Because the only thing he cares about seems to be his work. Even his tennis is work. I was just struck by that this morning—that he hardly even knows I'm there, except as someone to tell what to do. I mean, I'm not a stupid woman, and I hate it when he treats me like one, just dismisses what I have to say."

"Surely not, Iz. I know he just gets wound up in his work. That's all it is. Feeling the hot breath of young lions on his neck, no doubt. One of the pleasures of this profession is that you never have to suffer young lions. I mean, after Maddy died, I turned over the office practice to Spencer and Harrop, or most of it, and went into big animal work. You know why? I'd always liked big animals, and I was really impressed—I even feel silly telling *you* this—by Herriot's first book. That *All Creatures Great and Small*. I really liked the idea of being out and about, of having the mix of office and outside. So I could do it. Fix myself up with this buggy—my portable hospital—and just do it. Peter couldn't. He's been twenty years or more with Interchem, with ten to go. You know what I mean?"

"Yes, I guess so Rog. At least in my 'profession' I've sensed the breath of young lionesses from time to time. Not that I worry about it. I don't like it, either. But I don't worry."

Roger stopped for a light and lit his pipe. He thought for a minute about responding to that, but his instincts told him that anything he could say would only make it worse. She was right. He knew that well enough. Peter was as discreet as the next man, but no more so. The best thing to do was to change the subject.

"Now, about these pups. It's a litter of seven, five males and two females. I don't think you'd want to cope with a bitch, and two of the males are spoken for, so basically you'll be looking at three males. Evvy can tell you a good deal about the breed, of course, and there are several appealing things about it." He tromped the pedal and turned right. "As you'll see from the parents, these are smart, handsome dogs, big black fellows with heavy fur around the neck almost like a mane. From my point of view, one of the pluses is that they have a lot of the good points of a German shepherd without the bad things that come of careless breeding. The pedigree on these is one hundred percent free of hip dysplasia, for instance. Hateful thing, that, and it turns up a lot in the Germans. Nothing worse than buying a pup that seems to be free of it and then having to put him down when he's mature."

He shook his head, chomping down on his pipe.

"Anyway, I've had this bitch and dog for about four years. Both terrific animals, both with obedience degrees, absolutely devoted to the family. I don't have to tell you that their health is perfect. Evvy brings them in twice a year for checkups and worming, and their shots are current. They only breed them once a year, with the aim of having the pups ready to go to new owners in the spring. It's just a hell of a lot easier to get on with a pup if you bring him home when the weather is good, when walking him isn't a big chore and you can train him outdoors with a fair degree of regularity. By the time the rough weather rolls around, he's apt to be pretty well grown and pretty well trained."

Isabelle nodded. "Seems sensible. I know they're nice people. Responsible, too, I guess. That's good. But you know it's been so long since I've even looked at a pup that I don't know what to look for."

"Don't worry about it. These are all nice fellows, as far as I can tell, and perfectly sound, but you can't tell that much about a pup anyway. Of the three candidates, I'd guess you should just take the one that takes you, so to speak. Okay?"

"Rog, don't be exasperating. I said I didn't know if I'd want one, and I don't," she said.

"Who can resist a puppy?" he shot back with a grin. "I've never been able to, and I've been a vet for thirty years, for God's sake."

At that, they both laughed. It was too true. Roger always had a half-dozen animals around the place, at least—some for weeks, some for years. Madeleine had early on given up on keeping the house free of dog hair, and considered it clean if that was all there was visible. Isabelle realized that he'd made a special concession by not bringing along his traveling pack this afternoon.

They were past the Ox Ridge Hunt Club now. Roger steered left, and then left again, onto one of the back lanes, and pulled up in front of a blue split-level with black trim. Behind the house, Isabelle could see a high wire-mesh fence surrounding the yard, but it was apparently meant to keep wanderers out or puppies in, not to contain the Hutchinsons' dogs, for one of them was lying across the front door.

As the car stopped, he rose to his feet and assumed a confident stance, observing them squarely, his head up, his ears pricked forward, his tail low and motionless.

"Look at that, Izzy. He's wondering whether we're friend or foe, but he hasn't made up his mind yet. Stay in the car for a minute."

He rolled down the window on his side and called. "Brummel! Just me, old fellow, with a friend. Come on!" At the sound of Rog's voice, Brummel raised his head and began, very slowly, to wave his plumed tail. He trotted down the steps with a dignified air as they emerged from the car. Rog held out the back of his hand for Brummel to sniff, and then stroked his head. Isabelle followed his lead. "I'm relieved to see he likes us," she said. "He looks as though he could make short work of anyone if he didn't."

"I guess so. That's part of the purpose."

Evvy Hutchinson came to the door, waved, and called the dog to her.

"Brummel. Come!"

He turned abruptly, ran straight to Evvy,

stopped directly in front of her, and sat.

"Brummel. Finish!"

He came around to Evvy's left side and sat again.

"Down."

He lay down, resting slightly on one hip.

Evvy cupped her hand about an inch from his muzzle. "Stay," she said. He lay motionless as she strode toward them, tall and lanky, her black hair shining in the sunlight.

"How nice to see you both. It's been a long time, Isabelle, so come on in, and I'll fix us some coffee, and we can do some catching up while you look at the pups. How about you, Rog? Will you join us?"

"No thanks. I'm off to see the horses. Maybe when I get back, in about an hour, I think."

"Good. We'll see you then."

The two women waved to Rog as he barreled back down the road, then turned to walk back to the house.

Isabelle spoke. "That's very impressive, what you did with Brummel."

"Well, I work him every chance I get on most of the commands, just to keep him in practice. Rog probably told you that both Brum and Serena are obedience winners. She's made Companion Dog, Excellent and he has the next degree, Utility Dog, plus a tracking certificate. We train them ourselves, and I'd be glad to help you, if you want to try it."

"Well," said Isabelle, "I don't know about

that. I've never done it, but Peter trained our springer to hunt, and maybe he could do something if I decide to get a pup."

"Wouldn't work," said Evvy. "It's a matter of a little time every day. Consistency is the whole thing, really. We do it not just for trials but because they're genuinely better companions when they learn to respond to what you want and to what's really better for them. Besides, being a dog can be a pretty boring job, and this gives them something to do and a feeling of accomplishment. We've shown them in conformation, too. She's retired, now, but he only needs one more major win for his championship."

Indeed, Brummel was standing again, and Isabelle was struck by how beautiful he was. Evvy bent to stroke his shining mane. "Good dog, Brummel. Come on, and I'll let Serena out to play with you, so Mrs. Buckingham can see your offspring."

To Isabelle she said, grinning, "He's been feeling kind of left out. Just like new fathers everywhere, he thinks the old girl isn't spending enough time with him. He's always glad when the pups go home with their owners."

They went through the front door, down a long hall, to the kitchen, which was paved with newspapers. The kitchen table had been moved to one side to accommodate a large folding wire dog pen with a gate in one side, and a large box—lined with newspapers and padded with old bath towels—near the far wall. Serena, the bitch, had turned her back on the activities of the pups. Three were sleeping, two were mock-fighting, one had clambered onto his mother's back, and one was investigating a large water bowl with his feet.

As they entered, Serena rose and came to the gate. Evvy opened it and walked with the bitch to the front door, where Serena joined her mate with a cheerful bark. In a moment, Evvy was back.

"Let me bring out the three pups you'll be looking at," she said. "I'll leave the others in the pen."

Oh, damn! thought Isabelle. *Everyone's acting as though I'm going to take one of them for sure. What if I don't? Everyone's going to be just furious at me for putting them to all this trouble.*

Aloud, she said, "Fine. But how do you tell them apart?"

The puppies were no more than small, black, bearlike balls of fuzz, with stubby muzzles and lapped ears, none too steady on their feet.

"Oh, there are differences, even at this stage," said Evvy. "You know if you're around them a lot. The two males that are spoken for are the biggest, and that makes it easier." She bent over the wire and scooped up one puppy, setting it down gently on the papers, then did the same with a second and a third. That done, she sat down on the floor, letting the pups explore her hands and her blue jeans and sneakers. Isabelle, evidently expected to do the same, sat down next to her.

The largest of the three pups staggered off toward the pen and slumped over, sound asleep against the wire. The two smaller ones played at Evvy's side for a moment, and finally one wandered over to Isabelle. "That's the liveliest of the bunch," said Evvy. "He's actually the smallest, but he seems like a bright little guy."

The pup sniffed Isabelle's slacks and hands, nipped her fingers experimentally, and then clambered into her lap. "When you're that size," she laughed, "someone my size must seem like Mount Everest." She steadied him with her hand, and he sat down, looking up at her as if for some sign that she liked him. "Yes, little dog, I like you very much," she said. He yawned mightily, with a squeak, shook his head, and then pounced forward a bit, jumping up as though to get a closer look at her. In response, she lowered her face to him and stroked his back—soft and dark and silky. His bright button eyes were inches from her own, and he stretched out a pink tongue to her cheek.

"Aren't you just the sweetest little fellow?" she said. "Aren't you just?" He wriggled with pleasure. She set him down in her lap again. "And pretty, too," she added. "Nice puppy, pretty puppy." He felt warm and young and alive and friendly. There was something about him that was not just appealing, but reassuring as well. Almost like the sense of acceptance she'd tried to describe to Johnny. She rounded her shoulders to bring her face closer to his, and looked into his eyes.

"My husband thinks I should get a puppy. My daughter thinks I should get a puppy. Roger thinks I should get a puppy. Everyone does. I don't think I want a puppy, puppy, but what do you think? Hmmm? What do you think?" He pounced again, put one paw against her shoulder and licked her cheek.

"You think I should have a puppy, don't you, little fellow?" She stroked him again, ever so gently. He was so very small, so very clumsy. He dropped down into her lap again, and curled up to sleep. Obviously, he thought it was settled. The idea amused her. And he was a darling little thing. He'd be a fine big dog within a year, of course, but she would have lots to do to take care of him, and in time he'd be a good friend to have. Even a best friend. He couldn't replace Patch, of course. Nothing could. But now that he liked her, trusted her, how could she let him down? He'd picked her, after all. The sleeping weight in her lap, shifting slightly, testified to that.

"Well, Evvy, what can I tell you? He's a fellow who knows what he wants, and I seem to be it. I guess I will take him."

"That's terrific. I know he'll have a good home with you, and I'll be glad to help with him any way I can if you decide to show him or do obedience or anything. He's one of my favorites, and he took to you right away. He hasn't been friendly at all with other people who came to look, so you must be something pretty special. What do you want to call him? Before he's ready to go, I might at least be able to teach him his name."

Isabelle shrugged, trying to think. "I don't know. He's so pretty, and his father is Brummel. Maybe he should just be Beau."

"Beau it is, then. Now let me get you a cup of coffee, and you can either have it at the table or sit there on the floor with your Beau."

In moments, though, Beau had awakened, thoroughly refreshed by his nap, and gone in search of his brothers for a game of tag. This entailed bouncing on the sleepiest of them to wake him up, and then a good deal of bounding about, with occasional excursions to sniff around Isabelle's feet and solicit some patting and a few friendly words. Isabelle and Evvy sat at the table, chatting and enjoying the tumble of puppies around their feet and, when they grew too wild—not to say wet— back in the pen.

"I'm going to need some advice, you know," said Isabelle. "It's been fifteen years since I had a puppy in the house, and I'm sure that if puppies haven't changed, ways of dealing with them have."

"I'm sure you know all the basics, Isabelle. One suggestion I would make is that you get a folding wire dog crate. You can order one at the pet store. It helps a lot with the housetraining, at first, and it does get them used to being enclosed, in case you want to show them." She poured herself another cup of coffee from a pot that sat askew on the stove.

"I'll tell you what. I use a method of housetraining that really works quickly, and I got some paperbacks of the book I got it from, one for each pup and new owner. I'll get you one."

She put her cup down and disappeared toward the front of the house, and returned with a small paperbound book. "Here," she said. "This is *Good Dog, Bad Dog* by Mordecai Siegal and Matt Margolis. Matt's an absolutely terrific trainer, and the book has everything in it that you'll need in the first few months. Especially housetraining. I've done it this way and had them completely trained at eleven weeks."

Isabelle remembered how long it had taken with Patch, how long the kitchen floor had been papered over, how thoroughly exasperating it had been. "Great," she said. "I'll read it and try to get it down pat."

"And not just that," said Evvy. "With the rest of the book, I think you could take a dog to his first obedience degree, Companion Dog, before he's a year old. That really consists of things any housepet should do—heeling on and off lead, standing for examination, a one-minute sit-stay, a three-minute down-stay, and coming when called. Points are assigned to each exercise, and if you make 170 or better out of 200 in three different shows, you get the degree."

This was all new to Isabelle, and she said so. "Isn't that odd? I never knew there was such a thing, and I'm sure Patch could have done it easily. He would have enjoyed having a ribbon, I'm sure."

Evvy smiled at that. "Well, our dogs have been real showmen, and I do occasionally train for other people. Talk about ribbons! Come in the family room and I'll show you what they've won over the years." She stood up and led Isabelle down a short hall, at the end of which she threw open the door to the family room. One wall was covered with a large glass case that held ribbons in a rainbow of colors, silver plates and bowls, trophies, certificates, and medals.

"My God, Evvy. That's fantastic."

Back in the kitchen, Evvy let in Brummel and Serena, patting them fondly as she did so.

"I'm really startled by this training business, Evvy. How did you get started in it?" said Isabelle, freshening her own cup of coffee and glancing at her watch. Evvy had seated herself again, Brummel on one side, Serena on the other.

"Well, some years back, we had a German who was absolutely—or so we thought—uncontrollable. A pet shop pup. A really nice dog, but a maniac. I guess we didn't know what we were doing, because we could barely housetrain him, and we never could teach him to come or to stay or to stop chasing cars. Finally he was killed by one, up on the main road. We felt awful about it, but Rog told us that it really was our fault, that any dog was trainable if you knew how, and that it was the owner's business to learn how. He was right."

She paused for a minute, thinking back to the beloved shepherd that they'd failed.

"Anyway," she continued, "we went to a lot of shows, picked out Brummel, and started. Then we got Serena, and really started getting serious about it. I like the breed. These used to be called Groenendaels, and there's a ruddy variety called the Tervuren, and one more similar to a German shepherd called a Malinois. All guards and herders, very protective. They're tolerant of strangers, but basically they are one-family dogs. Sometimes they seem so smart that it's unnerving."

Isabelle glanced at Brummel, now stretched out peacefully on the floor, looking not in the least threatening. When she'd first seen him, as she and Rog had pulled into the driveway, he'd looked as if he'd tear out anyone's throat to protect his family. For some reason, the thought didn't bother her at all. To have a dog like Beau would mean that she, too, would have a pal and a protector. It made her feel oddly secure. She smiled.

"I'm sure that Beau and I will get along just fine, Evvy. He's a nice little fellow, though I know he won't stay little for long. When can I pick him up? And what do I owe you?" She reached for her handbag.

"He's weaned now," said Evvy, "but I think he's better off staying for a while. About three weeks, I guess. And he's two hundred dollars. You can pay me when you pick him up."

Isabelle shook her head. "No," she said, "let me do it now, and I can get him registered in the meantime. Can I come and see him every couple of days, so he'll get to know me?"

"Sure, I'm almost always here from two to three. Any time you want to come. I'll get the papers signed, since you need both our signatures. They'll be ready tomorrow. Why don't you bring Peter up to see Beau, and have a drink with us? About four? How would that be?"

Isabelle signed the check and handed it to Evvy. "Thanks, I'd like that," she said, "and I'm sure he will, too." She cocked her head. "Perfect timing, too! That must be Rog." There was the sound of an unmuffled motor, his heavy step on the porch, and then the doorbell. He opened the door and stuck his head in before Evvy could answer it.

"Come see my Beau, Rog," said Isabelle.

He scooped the puppy up from the floor of the pen, and handed him to Isabelle. "Well, I knew you couldn't resist. He's a sweetheart, isn't he? Did he pick you out?"

Evvy answered for her. "Walked right up to her and staked his claim," she said.

Isabelle held the tiny puppy to her cheek

and whispered, "I love you, Beau, and I'm going to come see you every day until you're big enough to come home. And in the meantime, I'll get everything ready for you." Then she put him carefully back in the pen and gathered her things together. As Evvy saw them out the door, Isabelle looked back. One of the pups—she thought it was Beau, but couldn't be sure—was standing with his front paws against the mesh and his nose pressed nearly through it. Feeling foolish, she blew him a kiss.

4

"Izzy, you'll never cease to surprise me," said Rog, as he dropped her off. "I felt a little resistance there for a while. But the first friendly puppy that crawls in your lap, and—bang!—before I can even get back you've written the check and committed yourself to another fifteen years of four-footed friendship."

Her astonishment showed. "Lord, Rog. Isn't that what you all wanted? And anyway, he picked me out. I know Peter will be pleased, and the kids, and I thought you would be."

"I am, darling, truly." He patted her hand for emphasis. "I'm only teasing. He's a swell pup, and you'll make out just fine. I just didn't know..."

Christ, how exasperating! she thought. *Someone urges you do something, and then you do it, and then they criticize you for doing it.* She smiled her best smile. "Look, one morning in that house without Patch was enough. I had to do it, and you know you thought it was the right idea. You suggested it. You even set it up. Right?"

"Sure, Izzy. Right. And this gives you three weeks to think it over and to get ready for him."

She held up the little paperback. "Evvy gave me this, and I'm sure I'll be well started. She offered to help, too."

"I guess she told you how she got started in obedience, and you ought to think about it. It's a good sport, and does nothing but good for the dogs. It's a lot of what being good to an animal is about, you know. That's what real love is, not coddling or treating a pet like a cross between a child and a fashion accessory. Know what I mean?"

"I guess so, Rog. But I'm not sure if it's for me."

"That's your decision, Izzy, but think about it."

"All right. But Rog, there's something I'd like you to think about, too. How about dinner on Sunday?"

He laughed. "Not going to think about that.

Just going to accept. How about that? Six-ish?"

"Perfect," she said, letting herself out of the car. "See you then."

And with a wave, he was gone.

She'd have to wait to tell John. And she didn't feel like talking to Anne. From somewhere inside her head, she could hear Anne's voice, saying something that meant, "I knew you'd do the sensible thing, Mother, if it were pointed out to you." That she didn't need. She'd save her news until Peter got home. Right now, she'd give herself an hour's nap, to make up for the night before. Then she'd have time for a long, luxurious bath, and putting herself together perfectly for their evening out.

By six-thirty, she stood in front of the mirror, checking carefully. *Not bad, for fifty-three. Old enough to be a grandmother, if kids got married anymore.* She wanted grandchildren, though Peter didn't. She'd asked him why, once, curious that it didn't seem to him as it did to her, like the completion of the cycle. He'd made a joke about it, but she hadn't thought it was funny. "It wouldn't be grandchildren that would bother me. It would be being married to a grandmother," he'd said. She could still feel the sting of that, somehow, the sense that Peter really believed that a woman, at a certain stage, was no longer attractive. It had been a long time since they'd made love. She couldn't remember, or didn't want to. Three months? Four?

She surveyed herself critically—the blue silk shirtwaist, the freshly shampooed hair. She dabbed a bit of Vent Vert on her throat and wrists. *Maybe tonight*, she thought. *No reason why not.*

At a few minutes to seven, she heard the distant wail of a commuter train, and at five after, Peter swung the Porsche into the driveway. She waved to him, through the kitchen window, for it was the habit of years that—on the nights he was home—the whistle of the train was her signal to go to the kitchen, dump a tray of ice into the ice bucket, and place a decanter of Scotch, a pitcher of water, two glasses, and the ice bucket on a tray to take into the study. There, they would have a drink or two before dinner; tonight it would be one, then one later in the restaurant.

"I'm home, Isabelle," Peter called from the front hall, as he hung up his coat. "Where're you?"

If she had not been there, waiting for him, it would have signaled something gravely out of place in their orderly lives, but this was part of the regular ritual.

"In the study, dear. Come on in and have a drink."

He brushed her cheek with his lips, absently, and then went to the makeshift bar. For her, he made a tall, light Scotch and water, for himself a shorter and stiffer one. Then he settled into his chair.

"So how did it go today? And how were the pups that Rog took you to see?"

"Well, the morning was rough, without Patch. But I did the usual things, and called the kids..."

"Called Annie in Chicago? At the office? I bet she loved that," he broke in.

"I thought she'd want to know, dear. I didn't mean to drag her out of a meeting and scare her to death, which I guess I did. She sent you a hug, though. Anyway, then Rog took me up to Evvy and Tom Hutchinson's to see the pups."

"And? How were they?"

Please don't criticize, she thought, swirling the ice in her glass for a moment, as she rehearsed a way of putting it that wouldn't make him believe he'd talked her into it. She took a sip.

"Well, you know I really thought that I wouldn't want one, but one of the smallest of them, a male, kind of took to me. Just clambered up into my lap and licked my face and fell asleep. So in three weeks, I'll have him. I'm calling him Beau."

Peter was bolt upright in his chair. Here it came. "My God, Isabelle, you must be kidding."

"Of course I'm not. Why should I be?"

"You said you didn't want one. That's what you said."

This really was annoying. "My goodness," she said, "I think I had this same conversation with Rog this afternoon. You two practically insist that I do something I didn't particularly want to do, and then when I decide that you were right after all, you suddenly question my judgment. I like this puppy. I even love this puppy. I paid for him already. What is the matter with you? I hope you don't treat your staff at the office this way."

Something rather like a snort escaped from Peter. "One, there's nothing the matter with me. Two, my staff at the office doesn't buy puppies with no consultation, and they run just fine on a combination of fear and greed. No, I'm not serious. I'm sure you've done the right thing, and I'm sure he's a fine puppy. He picked you out, didn't he?" She nodded. "Well, then," he continued, "the little fellow must have great taste. It's just that..." and his voice trailed off.

"Peter," she said, "I've had Patch for company all these years, and you and Rog were right. I need that sort of company, some sort of company. I really like this little Beau. You can meet him tomorrow. The Hutchinsons asked us for drinks. Okay? And I asked Rog for Sunday supper."

"It'll be nice to have Rog, but I'm not so sure about the Hutchinsons. What time do they want us? Bob and Zizi Roberts asked us, too. Bob did, anyway. I ran into him this morning."

Isabelle groaned. "Four at Hutchinsons'. What time at Robertses'?"

"Five-thirty or so," he said. "I know they're not your favorite people, but we both like Bob."

She giggled. "Right, we both like Bob, not that either one of us could say why. But *what* an impossible couple! How much did he touch you for this time?"

Peter looked embarrassed. "Only five," he said.

"What's he doing these days, anyway?" she asked.

"Oh, you know Bob. A little of this, a little of that, maybe nothing, maybe advertising or marketing or selling something. Poor bastard. He did say that Zizi is going into some boutique with Gina Poirier."

Gina was married to a network news anchorman, Anthony Poirier. They lived down the Point, and Zizi had been redecorating their house as they restored it, all at enormous cost and maximum inconvenience.

"Well, we've seen shops of that kind come and go in town as long as we've been here. Do you think they can make it go, Peter?"

He shrugged. "Who can tell? I'm sure they're capitalized properly, and that Tony would be the backer. That should help. And, as Bob always says, Zizi has an awful lot of talent. Gina must have great contacts, through Tony's work, so maybe so."

Isabelle tried, unsuccessfully, to suppress a

smile. "But do you remember the time, just after Annie moved to Chicago, that I thought we should spruce up the house, and I asked Zizi to do it? Do you remember?"

Clearly he did, for the recollection had caught him as he tried to swallow some of his drink, and the result was a choking spell, from which he emerged red-faced. "Christ, how could I forget? She came up here with all those damned drawings, and wanted to have us get rid of everything and buy all this stuff. Something about the clutter look. Clutter look! *They* certainly have it. I'll say that. She wasn't trying to foist anything off on us that she wouldn't live with herself." He shook his head ruefully. "That must be why poor old Bob is always stubbing his toes and falling over things. The clutter! The life-sized ceramic dog in the living room. The desk and the sofa and that big coffee table and all the bric-a-brac. Remember the time he cut hell out of himself? He put something down on one of those shelves, those glass things..."

"Étagère. It's called an étagère," Isabelle threw in, helpfully.

"Anyway, this little thing he put down literally broke its back and the whole thing came down, shattered all over the place." He shuddered at the memory. He'd driven Bob to the hospital that night to have the cuts stitched.

"This one time," said Isabelle. "This one time, for Bob. I'll call Zizi in the morning, to make sure that she thinks we're invited. Remember the time Bob asked you fishing off his dock for blues, and she locked the doors and wouldn't let you in the house to go to the bathroom? I never did know what that was all about."

At this, Peter was seized by a spasm of laughter that left him breathless. He was nodding, but he couldn't speak. When the laughter had subsided, he finished his drink and called to make their reservation, then slipped into his own coat and fetched for Isabelle the blonde mink that he'd bought her two Christmases before. He held it out for her, and hugged her to him to wrap the coat around her. "You're looking singularly pretty tonight, Isabelle," he said. "And I'm particularly pleased to see that the coat still matches your hair, or the other way around."

With something close to a bow, he offered his arm, ushered her out the door and down the path, and swept open the passenger door of the car with a grand gesture. *I think we've had a go at the bar car on the way home tonight,* she thought. Peter's courtliness, or his courtly moods, or whatever these episodes were, seemed to enter into some kind of equation with the level of alcohol in his blood. She tucked her hands into her pockets, and tried not to look as disappointed as she felt.

And sure enough, by the time dinner was over, Peter was growing quieter and sleepier by the minute. He declined a second cup of coffee, yawned widely, paid the check, and rose from the table. As he tucked her back into the Porsche, he even had a moment of unsteadiness, and, when they got back to the house, he turned to her, blinking gravely. "Isabelle, I'm awfully tired," he said. "Do you mind locking up? I'd just like to get to bed."

He looked old tonight, and tired. She told him that she did not mind. Not at all. After he had climbed the stairs, ever so heavily, she strolled to the windows of the living room and gazed out into the dark, over the water to the distant lights, and said, under her breath, "Why not, indeed?"

By the time she had turned out the lights and locked up, Peter was sound asleep, snoring lightly. But just before she slipped into bed, she remembered the clothes in the dryer. She tiptoed downstairs, folded them neatly into the laundry basket, and was in bed before it occurred to her that Peter had bought new underwear—the sort of shorts that looked like swimsuits. She did not ask herself why that might be.

5

The next morning dawned bright and sunny, and not just sunny but warm, a late winter day that seemed to have been borrowed from spring. Isabelle rose early, slipped into her robe, left her scuffs behind, and stopped in the kitchen for a quick cup of instant coffee. Then she rummaged for her pruning shears and a pair of sneakers. By the time Peter came down at eight, she was out at the side of the house, whacking away at the raspberry canes. The snicking sound of the shears led him to her.

"Isn't it a little early for that?" he said.

"No, the book says to do it this way, and I always have. I've never seen you turn down the raspberries. Rotten things, though. Fruit-bearing weeds is all they are. Look at this trash." She gestured to a tangled pile of discarded canes, then back at the plants, each of which had only three or four canes remaining.

"I didn't mean early in the year, Dizzy. I meant early in the morning," he replied. "How about rustling up some breakfast? I'm starved, and I'd love a cup of coffee."

She shrugged, and handed him her shears. "Okay, my helpless friend. I'll come on in."

In minutes, she'd tossed together some breakfast and sat down with Peter at the kitchen table. Polishing off the last of his eggs and muffin, he pushed his plate back. "Got anything special that I should do today?" he asked.

"Yes, come to think of it. If you're playing this morning you could take the wagon and pick up a couple of bags of mulch. Can you do that?"

"Sure. I told Charlie MacDougall that if the weather held I'd make up to him, in spades, for taking a couple of sets away from me in the last tournament. Guess I'd better call him. We set up for ten o'clock." He started to make for the telephone, but she stopped him.

"Charlie MacDougall is thirty-four," she said gently. "He has twenty-one years on you, dear. Please take it easy."

He folded his arms across his chest, cocked his head, and raised an eyebrow at her. If the pose was lighthearted, his words were not. "So bloody what, Isabelle? My game's damned near as good as it was. And besides, when you can't be a lion anymore, you can be a fox. And that's what I am: a fox. A silver fox, I'll admit, but a fox nevertheless."

Against this—pride, vanity, competitiveness, whatever it was—she could do nothing. No logic could penetrate. "Okay, but don't forget the mulch, and remember that you should be back by three to change."

With a winner's smile, he said, "Sure. Fine. And if you need something to worry about, worry about the fenders on the Porsche, all right?" And he tossed her the keys.

Shortly before ten, Peter was out the door on the way to his tennis date, and Isabelle was finishing her housework. She drew her shopping list, tomorrow's dinner in mind. Chicken fricassee from the complicated Julia Child recipe. Rice and green salad, and white wine. Early strawberries for dessert. She'd need most everything else, but, given the size of the cellar, Peter had ample wine. It would be festive, she'd make sure of that. She finished her list and started off on her errands, being very careful with the Porsche.

She began her cooking when she got home, laying out the ingredients for the fricassee rather than putting them away. It took, always took, hours to make, but it was delicious, and smelled absolutely heavenly as it simmered. Everything was ready and waiting in the refrigerator by the time Peter returned at three. She could hear him sniff the air as he came through the door. "Sneaky woman," he laughed. "You're after my waistline again. You're trying to give the cardiologist a heart attack. You've laid on some fricassee."

"Not for tonight, dear. For tomorrow. Don't be disappointed," she said.

But he was, obviously. "I have to wait?"

"Yes, you do. We've got steaks and salad for tonight, so you can ruin your regime tomorrow. So pop upstairs and change instead of being so spoiled. Who won, anyway?"

"Who else? The old silver fox himself, naturally." If he was trying to look modest, the attempt failed utterly, and he bounded up the stairs so lightly that she was struck by the contrast with the night before. *The silver fox, indeed,* she thought, shaking her head. She had never played tennis, not since she'd married Peter, anyway. He had been a virtuoso, and she was, figuratively speaking, just on the scales. It would have irked him and humiliated her if she'd ever tried. Sometimes she'd resented the game, the time it took, the time it took away from her, but when it made him feel this good, it made her feel good, too. She just wished that she could have the same rejuvenating effect on him as winning a match seemed to.

She caught herself and corrected. He'd won this one against a much younger man. And the chances were—she knew they were, had harbored the signs, had hunted for more—that a different kind of match with a much younger woman would have had the effect that nothing with her ever would, ever again. She did not like to think of the nights she'd sat in the study with Patch, painstakingly working on a piece of needlepoint, watching a bit of television, wondering where Peter was and whom he was with. He was effectively single a good deal of the time, and so, she guessed, was she. Single in a place that was made for families, for couples. When was the last time she'd met any new people? Gina and Tony Poirier? Two years ago? She wondered what other women did in these circumstances, if there was anything that could be done.

"Say, Iz?" Peter called, interrupting her thought.

"Yes, dear."

"The mulch is in the garage." He paused. "And Iz? Did you call Zizi?"

"No, I forgot. Shall I do it now?"

"Don't bother. I'll do it from upstairs."

"Well, Isabelle, I'm expecting great things of this pup of yours," said Peter as they set off for the Hutchinsons'. It was close to four, and clouding over again as they left; Isabelle wiggled down into the collar of her coat.

"I'm not sure about great things, but he likes me, anyway. And he's a nice pup, Peter. I'm sure you'll like him."

"And what's this trials thing?"

"I'm not sure I understand that yet, but they can explain it, I know. You should see the trophies they have. They're really into it."

"Sounds like a good thing, not a bad thing for you, if you'd do it. The pup probably has some aptitude for it, and you have all kinds of time to work with him. Do you good—getting out and meeting some new people and all." The patronizing tone was back in his voice, and Isabelle felt a prick of resentment. Why should she be assigned a dog for company and dog shows for entertainment? To make it easier for him to go his own way? What ever happened to having a shared existence?

Rather than respond, she fumbled in her handbag for the pack of cigarettes she'd bought that morning. She stripped the wrapper back, pulled one out, and lit it.

"Smoking? Really, Isabelle, when did you start that again?" Peter's disapproval floated like the smoke itself between them.

"Yesterday," she said, trying to sound unapologetic. "I had two. It's really been a rough couple of days."

"You know I hate it."

"I'm sorry. I'll stop again soon. I can keep it down, you know. I never did smoke that much." Was there anything more hateful than having to apologize to keep the peace?

"You shouldn't smoke at all, and you know it. It's your life, Isabelle. Also your lungs and your heart and your complexion. But if you don't care, what business is it of mine? As long as you don't leave ashes and butts around, fine. Please don't use the ashtray. I hate a smelly, dirty car."

She felt herself tighten another notch. "Peter, please lay off. We're almost there."

And so they were, making the two lefts past Ox Ridge and pulling into the driveway without another word, save directions. Tom, coming down the front steps, had Brummel with him. Peter turned to her, his eyes wide. "Christ, is that the kind of dog you bought?"

"Well, yes, of course it is. What did you think a Belgian shepherd was?"

"I don't know," he replied, evidently confused. "I had in mind something more like a collie—Albert Payson Terhune and all that. Not a big wicked-looking black police dog kind of thing."

It seemed uproariously funny to her, and she laughed for a long moment as they were getting out of the car. "Well, mine's little yet, and they aren't wicked at all. Don't worry about it."

Now Tom was shaking Peter's hand heartily, and saying, "Hi, Peter. Isabelle. Come on in the kitchen. I'll let Serena out and you can play with Beau."

Serena joined Brummel in the back yard, as Tom bustled around with drinks, everyone stepping cautiously to avoid the pups as Evvy tried to scoop them up, all but Beau, and return them to the pen. But even before that, one broke away from his littermates, lurched over to Isabelle, and sat down in front of her, tail wagging expectantly, tongue lolling, eyes alight with eagerness.

"Is that Beau?" said Peter.

"Damned if it isn't," Tom replied. "He's seen Isabelle once in his life, and he seems to know exactly who she is."

Slowly, Isabelle crouched down to the pup and held her hand out to him.

"Beau? Hi there, little fellow. I really am your person, right? Come here. I'd like you to meet Peter."

She'd been about to pick him up, but the little dog, still seated, turned his head sharply toward Peter, with an air of dignity, almost of appraisal.

"Yes, that's Peter," she said. "Go see Peter."

Beau looked back at her, turned, and walked to Peter. He stood in front of him with the same solemn air as before. Peter crouched down, as Isabelle had, extending his hand to the pup, clearly expecting him to respond. "I'm glad to see he's not as formidable as his dear old dad," he said with heavy humor. "I guess if you watch them grow you get accustomed to their looks." But his hand was still extended, as Beau looked inquiringly at Isabelle.

"Isn't he funny?" Evvy chimed in. "He seems to be waiting for a word from you, Isabelle."

"Oh, I doubt that. But go ahead, Beau. Meet Peter," she said.

With that, the little dog bounded toward the outstretched hand, sniffed at it, and then rolled over on his back in an invitation for Peter to rub his belly. But when Peter touched him, Beau went for his hand, and sank his tiny teeth in it. Peter bellowed, not so much in pain as in surprise, and jumped to his feet, sucking his hand. "Christ, he bit me! Hurt, too. Christ!" He sucked at it some more, and Evvy, obviously perplexed, grabbed a tin of Band-Aids from the cupboard and, taking his hand, plunged it under the tap.

"Lord, Peter, I'm sorry," she said. "They're

teething, of course, and just seem to gnaw on anything. I'm sorry it was you."

Isabelle, who had watched the whole performance, was startled, but with a tinge of malicious glee. It seemed so fitting, somehow, after the way he'd talked to her in the car. And it couldn't be anything serious. He was just carrying on. "You know he couldn't possibly have meant it, dear. Let me have a look," she said. He held it out, the two tiny red marks each oozing just a drop of blood at the base of the thumb.

"Nothing to fuss about, Isabelle. I was surprised, really. That's all," he said. He looked a bit embarrassed for having fussed anyway. As Evvy put the last of the elusive pups into the pen, Isabelle lifted Beau up, kissed him on the end of his shiny nose, and seated herself in a kitchen chair, settling the little dog into her lap.

Tom, papering over an awkward pause by presenting them each with a drink, invited Peter to join him in the back while he put Brummel through his paces. The two women watched through the window as the big dog went through the repertoire of heeling, standing, staying in the sit and down positions, coming when called, and some spectacular retrieving over long and high jumps. In the fading light, Isabelle was struck not by the performance, but by the unity between the man and the animal, their perfect responsiveness to one another. At the finish, Tom put his arms around Brummel, stroking his glossy black coat and ruffling his pointed ears. It was like the gesture one made with a favorite child.

Even Peter was impressed, full of questions about how long the training had taken and the like. Ever the quantifier, he asked to see the trophies, and trooped off happily to the family room with Evvy and Tom. Isabelle could hear them—Peter exclaiming over one thing or another, Tom explaining, Evvy filling in. But Isabelle's fingers moved lightly along the snoozing pup's side, soft and shining, warm against her lap. She turned to watch Serena and Brummel, romping gaily in the backyard. Yes, they were fine animals, beautifully trained, in peak condition, but she liked her Beau. "Some day, little fellow," she whispered, "you're going to be a great big furry animal like that. But now you're just a little stout wobbly guy. And that's just how I like you. Sharp teeth and all."

As she spoke to him, he stirred slightly, gave forth a great, yawping yawn, and snuggled harder against her, with an absent lick at the hand that held him close.

All too soon it was five-fifteen, and time to leave. Reluctantly, Isabelle cuddled Beau to her one last time before handing him gently to Evvy, and promising her that she'd return on Monday. Then Evvy fetched the forgotten papers, which Isabelle stuffed in her coat pocket, and they were back in the car.

She turned to Peter. "Well, what did you think?"

"I think it'll be fine, Dizzy. I really do.

Imagine having an animal like that—handsome, perfectly trained, all that. And the trophies! I have to admit I'm impressed."

"I mean Beau, Peter."

"Well that's what I mean. If he's a chip off the old block, he should be quite a guy. Can't tell much right now, of course," he said.

Damn! she thought, her anger rising again. *How he does focus on the wrong thing.*

"Peter, for heaven's sake. I mean that since he's the dog that we're going to have, it would be helpful if you liked the puppy rather than just the accomplishments of his parents. So I am asking you what you think of Beau." Her voice came out perfectly flat and perfectly even; she had banished from it both her anger and the tears that she felt, suddenly and irrationally, to be welling up inside her.

Peter, incredulous, jerked to an abrupt halt and turned to stare at her. "My lord, Isabelle, it's just not like you to go all menopausal on me. What's the matter with you? I like him fine. I could do without his goddamn sharp teeth, and I can hope he doesn't grow up with some kind of a mean streak, but I like him fine. What's not to like? He's your dog, anyway." He started the car again.

"I think he's really special," she whispered.

Peter didn't answer until they turned down Ring's End Road toward the Robertses', and then he reached out awkwardly to pat her arm. "If we're fighting, I don't know why, but I'm sorry," he said. "Now come on, and let's try to have a good time, okay?"

She nodded mutely, feeling foolish and unaccountably guilty. And then they were at the Robertses'.

Bob greeted them with hectic enthusiasm, with a drowning-man handshake for Peter and an extravagant kiss on the cheek for her. Zizi stood behind him, a Maltese terrier under each arm, peering rather anxiously over the tops of her glasses and through the half-lit, fashionable disorder of her living room. It had been photographed for *House & Garden* two years before, and now, seemingly frozen by the click of a shutter, looked exactly the same—each bibelot in place, each fabric-covered matchbox, each basket of dried flowers. It was the product of Zizi's perfect taste, of her infinite capacity for taking pains.

Zizi herself was tiny, chic, looking no more than thirty-five if the light were kind. In fact, she was fifty, and sometimes, even in the kindest light, the hardships showed. As Isabelle had once inadvertently discovered, Bob's summer glass of iced tea was apt to be brim-full of Jack Daniels rather than Thomas Lipton, which couldn't have made things any easier for the Robertses. Right now he was holding a glass of tomato juice that was more probably a stiffish bloody mary, and Isabelle wished she could be anywhere else. Something was going to go wrong. She could feel it coming.

Stupidly, inadvertently, in the midst of telling them about her Beau, she passed some kind of remark about how she'd always preferred big dogs. Zizi had taken it personally, was taut and ready to snap anyway, responded shrilly and with an air of injury. Nothing could salvage the evening after that, and Isabelle grabbed the first available break in the conversation—once, indeed, it had resumed—to rise and say that they must be going.

"God damn it, Isabelle," Peter snapped when they were in the car. "I don't much enjoy it either, but why did you have to make a remark like that? That kind of thing's just embarrassing."

"No point, Peter. Just a slip, that's all," she said wearily. "Zizi's touchy about too many things anyway. If I put you in an awkward spot, I'm sorry, but let's just go home."

As she fixed supper, Peter settled rather grumpily in the study with his Mozart tapes on the deck and the *New Yorker* on his lap. A fresh drink was by his side. She served supper on small tables in front of the fireplace, but they ate in a silence broken only by the music. *Well,* she thought, as she washed up the dishes, *he can sit there and sulk all night as far as I'm concerned. I'll go up and read.* But as she paused on her way to bed to say good night, he looked up from his magazine and said, "Don't go up yet, Dizzy. It's still early. I'll pull your needlepoint frame around for you and you can sit with me awhile. How would that be?"

The frame, an antique that he'd bought somewhere near Charleston on one of his trips, was of mahogany, with baskets for wool built into gracefully turned supports. To some extent unwieldy, it was still, as Peter had said when it arrived, a beautifully feminine piece of furniture. Isabelle always felt like quite the Victorian lady when she sat down to work at it.

Tonight, as Peter pulled it around before her chair, the frame held needlepoint canvas outlined with odd shapes, within which grew an intricate, flamelike pattern that shaded from the palest cream to the deepest gold. It was Isabelle's largest project so far, for the dozen odd shapes—once assembled—would go to reupholster Peter's beloved wing chair. In a few months' time, its stained brown leather would be replaced with perfect color.

As Isabelle settled into her own, smaller chair—the twin of his in every way but size—she thanked him for moving the frame. In moments, she was caught up in her work, dazzled, as she often was, by the rhythmic beauty of the colors rising, falling, blending, shading. It was like music, like Peter's Mozart, which was what she'd had in mind when she'd planned the project.

So far, it had taken about six months of intermittent work, and there remained only the pieces for the wings to complete and the piece for the back, which was largest of all. A lot of work, but when the chair was redone, completely refinished and reupholstered, welted in gold leather, all the effort would seem worth it.

She threaded her needle and worked, with the absent perfection of long practice, another rising and falling line of color across the canvas. As she paused to thread a long length of wool, she looked up at Peter.

"Do you like it, dear?" she said. She knew she'd said that too many times. If she hadn't known, Peter's sigh, preceding his reply, would have told her so.

"You know I do," he said abruptly.

"It's taking ages, I'm afraid. But it shouldn't be much longer."

"Not in any hurry, are we?" he said, rattling the magazine a bit.

"No, I guess not. Didn't mean to interrupt you."

For an hour the only sounds were of the pop-slap of wool against canvas, the rustle of a magazine page, the music from the Mozart tape. When it ran out, Isabelle yawned and, putting down her work, stretched. "Ready for bed?" she said.

He shook his head. "No, you go ahead. I'm going to finish what I'm reading. Be up in a little while."

What could she do? Ask him? Say "please"? She had more pride than that left, anyway.

She could still hold on to that, could still pretend that nothing was wrong. So she kissed him good night and went upstairs.

6

Sunday, the clouds had cleared again, and the day was scented with spring. Though the trees were still bare, the willows had turned a pale shade of gray green that predicted their leafing out within days. The daffodils and forsythia were in bud, if not yet in bloom, and the crocuses were pushing up in the lawns by ones and twos and threes.

Saturday's strains seemed to pale in the clear light from the sky and the Sound. The day, as she said to Peter over an early cup of coffee, put her in a party mood, even though Rog would be their only guest. Peter could pick up some flowers for the table when he went for the paper. While he was gone, Isabelle brought down all her best china and silverware, her finest linens, her most fragile glassware, and by the time he returned, the table was done, lacking only the early blue iris and daffodils he'd picked up for the centerpiece. Isabelle glowed with pleasure as they sat down to their waffles and coffee, and rummaged good-naturedly for the sections of the Sunday *Times* that she most wanted.

"I asked John and Alison for supper, but they couldn't make it. Maybe next week. I do wish they'd get married, though. For one thing, it's hard to describe. And for another, I really would love to have at least one grandchild," she said.

"Alison doesn't exactly strike me as the motherly type," Peter said.

"I guess not, but..."

Peter gave her a wolfish grin. "It would make me feel old, and I'm not feeling particularly old at the moment. Look, I'm not due on the courts until noon. It's ten-thirty now, and I'll even clean up the dishes afterward. Want to play honeymooners?"

"But I haven't even bathed yet, Peter," she said.

"Do I care?" He finished his coffee. "You can do that while I clean up down here. Rog won't even be here until six."

They left the dishes on the table and went upstairs. These occasions, she felt, were too rare and too important to pass up, even though she disliked the idea of playing honeymooner, disliked the idea of pretending to be what they so obviously were not, could not understand why what they really *were* could not be as pleasing—in its way. She could not put it into words, would not have if she'd been able to find them, but she was offended.

Did it matter? Maybe everyone had to cope this way, or in much worse ways. Was she picky, maybe crazy? Should she say something about it, or try? Women, some women anyway, could do that these days. But she could not, hadn't the experience with it, had all the wrong habits.

Afterward, washing up the breakfast dishes, Peter was annoyed at himself. At Isabelle, too, but mainly at himself. He rinsed a plate and stuck it in the dishwasher. He didn't have anything to say to her anymore, didn't enjoy her anymore, and now, on top of the whole thing, she thought she could fool him by faking. What the hell? He'd take the trip to Atlanta this week and pick somebody up. In Atlanta and Tucson and Palm Beach—maybe anywhere that you picked up a woman for a night or two—you could make it perfect and nobody insulted you by faking. It didn't have to carry thirty years of all that marriage was—middle age, and widening distance, and dead dogs.

He snapped the last dish into the dishwasher, shut it, and took the sponge to the table and counters. His annoyance, shoved to one side, would stay to one side until he was off again. By the time he poured himself another cup of coffee and settled down with another section of the paper, he was fine.

Isabelle, soaking happily in a warm tub, felt serene. She wiggled her toes, thinking that if only Peter could have waited, she might have been more in the mood, would have felt more attractive and responsive. *Oh well. A little faking never hurt anything.* By the time she'd dressed, changed the bed, and bundled the laundry into the machine, Peter was getting ready to leave. Smiling, she touched his hand. "Will you be back by four, dear?" He nodded in affirmation, concentrating not on her but on selecting a racket from the press in the laundry room. He swung one in a tentative sort of way, and winced.

"What's the matter?" she asked.

"Don't know. The thumb hurts a little, and the Band-Aid is awkward as hell."

"Why don't you soak it in salt water for a while, and I'll put some bacitracin on it and rebandage it?"

"No time, Isabelle. Got to get there, or I'm going to be late." And with that, he gathered his things together and left.

But he was home by two, looking downcast. His hand had bothered him, he said, and he'd lost his match in straight sets. Isabelle could hear the shower running for a full twenty minutes after he went upstairs, and it was another half hour before he came down. "Look at my hand, will you?" he said, holding it out. The puncture marks seemed reddish, though the tiny wounds were healing over.

Turning the hand to the light to make certain, she suggested again that he soak it and then rebandage it. "It doesn't seem quite right, but I think it's more the way it went into the muscle than an infection," she said, as she drew the hottest water possible from the tap and tossed in some salt. "I guess we're lucky it wasn't Brummel that took a fancy to your hand."

She'd meant it as a joke, but it didn't go over. Peter sat in silence at the kitchen table, holding onto the magazine section with his left hand, dipping his right into the water for a few seconds at a time until it had cooled enough to be bearable. Rather than flutter, or simply watch him sulk, Isabelle decided on a walk, not down to the beach, but up to the end of the Point to look at the new construction that was transforming the former property of the Convent of the Sacred Heart into something far too posh to be called a development. She went upstairs and slipped into her loafers, and then, on her way out, stuck her head through the kitchen doorway.

"I'm going for a walk, dear, but before I go, I did want to remind you to bring up some wine," she said.

He pulled his hand out of the soaking solution. "Christ, I'm sorry. Clean forgot about it. Pinot chardonnay, all right? California, since you've been smoking again?"

"Sure. Fine with me."

"I'll get it now, then," he said, wiping his hands on a clean towel.

He rose and went to the living room, from one wall of which the "new" cellar stairs had been installed to parallel those that went up to the second floor. A door to the stairs, cleverly concealed in the paneling, had superseded an older trapdoor-and-ladder affair, and allowed safer, simpler access to the cellar, though they used it only for storing Peter's wines. In a few moments he returned, toting a single bottle of Wente Brothers, which he set to cool in the bottom of the refrigerator. By then, Isabelle was walking briskly down the Point, her head down, concentrating on blanking from her mind the irritants of the last three days. She'd make it a pleasant evening. With Rog coming, it would be easy. One of the few things that could still give her the old sense of peace and fitness was to have an old friend—or better yet, the family—around the dining room table, to have Peter in his chair and she in hers, the table beautifully appointed.

By the time she came home, her mood had lightened, and so had Peter's. The hand felt better, no question about it, and she took care to be extra solicitous as she rebandaged it. He sat with her in the kitchen as she prepared the salad, boned the chicken, and measured out the rice. In no time, it seemed, Rog had arrived, two of his dogs on his heels, a gift bottle of Scotch under his arm. No wonder he'd been such a popular extra man since Maddy died! He was, quite simply, the sort of man who was born to be a good guest, full of stories about his profession, willing to laugh at anyone's jokes, so good-hearted and so entertaining that an evening with him was always too short. He teased Isabelle about Beau, Peter about having been "savaged," as he put it, by a junior hound of the Baskervilles—or at least the Hutchinsons. The evening floated by, enhanced by the whiskey and wine, the good food and the banter. As he left, it seemed to Isabelle as though it had gone by all too quickly.

Afterward, lingering over each task, Isabelle straightened up and put everything away. When she'd finished, she sneaked a cigarette in the kitchen, savoring the smoke, enjoying a moment of doing something Peter disliked without his knowing about it, already missing the feel of having a guest in the house, the moment of festivity.

"Isabelle?"

She thrust the cigarette under the tap and tossed the damp butt in the garbage pail.

"Yes, dear. In the kitchen."

He leaned into the swinging door from the dining room. "What are you up to?" he said. "I thought I'd start a fire if you wanted to sit in the study for a while. I'll fix another cup of coffee for myself, and one for you if you'd like."

She shook her head. "No coffee for me, but a fire would be nice."

"You go on in, then," he said. "I'll be right back with the wood." He started through the laundry room into the garage, where the wood was kept. The log carrier swung lightly from his left hand.

Behind him, Isabelle propped the door for him as she went through to the dining room. She paused there, picking up the centerpiece from the table, and took it with her into the study, where she placed it carefully on the desk, well back from the fire. Peter had already pulled her needlepoint frame into place, and, as she sank down into her chair, she was grateful for that. Suddenly, she was tired, and her feet ached. She kicked her shoes off and threaded a strand of gold wool into her needle.

In moments, Peter was back and had occupied himself with building the fire, fiddling with paper, fatwood, the draft. Soon it was blazing. He dusted off his hands, resumed his seat, and peeled back the bandage on his hand. Turning the thumb to catch the light, he said, "Damn thing hurts again, but it looks all right, don't you think?" He held it out for her to look, but she couldn't really see it very well.

"I guess so," she said. "Do you want to soak it some more?" He made a face and shook his head.

"Don't feel like it right now. It's all right, I guess. What are you going to be doing this week?"

"Oh, I'm not sure. I should probably shop for Beau. You know, get everything ready for his homecoming. And I'll drop in and see him.

And call the kids sometime during the week. Maybe I'll go into the city and have lunch with Johnny. Something like that. Nothing special, I suppose. What about you?"

"Atlanta, you mean? Oh, the usual going over. Budget preparation and that. It's getting to be spring down there, so I think I'll play a little. Nice people down there, and it's become a beautiful city—very progressive. What do you need for Beau, anyway?" he said, regarding his hand. "I mean besides a muzzle?"

"Really, don't you think you're making an inordinate fuss, Peter?" she said, pausing for effect, to let him know just how irked she was by all this harping. "Otherwise, a few things. A dog crate, Evvy says. A pad for that, I guess. Dishes. Food. Some toys. A nylon slip collar. A half-inch, six-foot leather lead. A slip-chain collar for later. A rubber curry brush and a wire slicker brush. Hot water bottle. Clock. Vitamin supplement and heartworm medicine. It sounds like a lot, but it's mostly little stuff," she said.

"Told you we should have kept some of Patch's things."

This was no time to come back at him. She stitched for a while, and then made an effort to get off on another subject.

"Rog is a darling, isn't he? I'm sure half the single women in town have set their caps for him. He certainly meets enough of them, between the practice and the parties he's invited to. I wonder if he'll ever marry again."

"Not if he's smart, he won't," said Peter. "It seems to me that Rog probably has it wired. Plenty of attractive women, but basically his own life, the way he wants it. No ties. Perfect."

"But it's not perfect, Peter," she protested. "For years, he had a happy marriage to a lovely woman. I'd think he'd want that again. I'd think anyone would. Wouldn't you?" She finished off a thread in the back of the work and paused.

"Oh, who can tell what he'd want? I really can't speak for anyone else. God knows, no one understands anyone else's marriage. Damned few people even understand their own," he said.

"What's that supposed to mean?"

"Speaking in general, Isabelle, speaking in general. Not us, Dizzy. I mean, in thirty years we've had a cross word or two, and some hard work, but never anything really wrong, no bad times, not really. Right?"

But Isabelle was stitching again, the wool making small popping sounds as she pulled each stitch tight. Too tight. He took her silence for agreement.

7

Peter had gone to Atlanta, and the week lay empty before her, as empty as the house was. In an hour of cleaning the place was spotless. Then what? She had no grocery shopping to do, and there was nothing else she needed. It would be two o'clock before she could go up to see Beau. All right. At least she could shop for him.

First she found her coat and fished out the registration papers, which she made out carefully and tucked into an envelope with a check made out to the American Kennel Club. Then a shopping list of dog supplies. Most of it was to come from the pet shop. On her way there, she mailed the papers, and then found a parking place near the rickety building that housed the shop. She managed—lingering selectively over each item—to kill nearly an hour and to find everything but the food and the crate, which she ordered and paid for on the promise of a Thursday pickup. She wrote a check for the purchases, and lugged them to the car. Then she went to the supermarket, a task that took her another forty minutes of reading labels on bags and cans before she filled her cart and wheeled it to the checkout.

On the way home, she stopped at Rog's hospital for some heartworm drops, and stayed to be introduced to a rather formidable woman named Ellen O'Toole, who'd apparently moved into the cottage two doors north of the Robertses. Miss O'Toole seemed goodhearted, if her treatment of her small cairn terrier was any indication, but brusque and spinsterish. Isabelle found something disquieting about her—a certain dourness, a stance that indicated she was somehow on the offensive. A terrier of sorts herself, perhaps. Before a break in the conversation, she'd managed to tell Isabelle not only that her cairn was a proven obedience winner and that obedience was "no game for amateurs, my dear, no game at all," but also that—as was perfectly clear by then—she herself was a woman who always, "but always," spoke her mind.

Saying goodbye to Rog, Isabelle leaned over and whispered to him, "No young lions, dear, but plenty of old dragons, it seems!" He laughed heartily at that, and shrugged his shoulders.

Home again, she had everything put away by around one. After a quick lunch, there was not too much time left before she could leave for the Hutchinsons'. She'd looked forward to it ever since Saturday, and sang along with the radio in the car on the way there. It was exactly two o'clock as she turned into the driveway, and she was obscurely pleased at the perfect timing.

Since it was fairly warm and dry, Evvy suggested that she take Beau outdoors. She seated herself in a sunlit patch of grass, wiggling her fingers at Beau, who pounced again and again, emitting what might have been a bark, had it had a slightly longer distance to travel. Finally, worn out, he climbed into her lap and nuzzled against her.

"It's all right, Beau, isn't it? Just you and me and the sunshine."

On his left side, she could feel the lub-dub of his tiny heart, and where she rested her hand, his soft breath was warm against it.

"Well, little fellow," she continued, "I've got to tell you that I wish you could come home. I'm all by myself right now, and I'm lonesome. I have two big children, but they're never home anymore. And Peter went to Atlanta. He's gone a lot anyway. So there I am in that big old house. Hmmmm? When do you think you can come? I did your shopping, and I'm all ready for you."

Beau stretched, yawned, and tumbled to the ground, where he righted himself and gave a great, uncoordinated shake. "What's up?" she said.

But instead of coming back, he trotted toward the gate in the chain link fence. Isabelle followed, responding to the occasional backward glance from him. It seemed to her to be a sort of "come on" look, and the thought amused her.

When they reached the fence, she looked down at him as if for a sign of some sort. "Okay, Beau, what did you want me to see?"

she said. He looked up at her and whimpered. Whatever it was he seemed to want her to see, all that was in view was her own car in the drive. He tried the bark again.

"What, Beau? Bird? Rabbit? Squirrel? What?"

Nothing.

She picked him up and carried him up the steps to the kitchen door. It was nearly three, and she did not want to overstay her welcome, so she gave his back a last fond nuzzle before she opened the door and took him back in the house. But he whimpered softly as she placed him back in the pen with his littermates, and more loudly as she picked up her bag and prepared to leave. Evvy appeared in the front hall.

"What's he crying for?" she asked.

"Nothing that I can think of," said Isabelle. "I guess it's too nice a day, and he just didn't want to come in."

"I doubt it's the weather. More likely the company. Anyway, it won't be long until he can go home with you, and he'll have the whole place to himself with no competition."

"I'm ready when he is," said Isabelle. "I went shopping this morning and got all the stuff."

But now the pitch of his whimpering had risen, and the sound of entreaty was unsettling. "Look, I'd better just get going. I'll see you tomorrow," she said, and half ran to her car.

On the way home, she remembered two things she'd forgotten even to put on her list, the hot water bottle and the alarm clock. She stopped at the pharmacy for them and then, remembering that she had a long evening to pass, browsed in the bookstore next door until a couple of things took her fancy. By the time she got back to the house, it was nearly half past four. The phone was ringing—she could hear it from the garage—and kept ringing until she picked it up.

"Isabelle, is that you?" The voice on the other end was breathless, and behind it she could hear a strange, high keening sound. It took her a minute to realize that the voice belonged to Evvy.

"Listen, I don't know what to do about this, but you know how Beau was whimpering when you left?"

"Yes, sure."

"Well, right after you left, it got worse. He's not hurt or anything. But he's been howling for an hour and a half. He's got the dogs upset, and the puppies are frantic. And I'm absolutely at the end of my rope. Listen. I'll hold the phone up."

The sound grew louder, more piercing, and then Evvy spoke again.

"I don't know what to do," she said.

Isabelle could only think he must be hurt. "Have you called Rog?" she asked.

Exasperation was creeping into Evvy's voice. "I tell you, there's no reason to, Isabelle.

There's just nothing wrong with him. I'm telling you. Nothing. Look, this may be crazy, but from the timing of it, I think he wants you. Can you come?"

"Certainly I can. I don't know that it'll do any good, but I can be there in fifteen minutes." Once off the phone, she grabbed her bag and ran.

As she got out of the car, Isabelle could hear it, a high wail between a whimper and a howl, the sound of something trapped. But by the time Evvy had opened the door, it had eased off. Evvy looked frantic, hanging against the door, weakly gesturing for her to come in. "God, did you hear it?" she said.

"Yes, but it's stopped now. Where is he?" She peered down the hall to see him standing with his forefeet braced against the side of the pen.

"Come on. Let's go get him," said Evvy, standing aside. "I'm just so glad it's stopped. Unnerving. I think he did want you. He's fine now that you're here. My God! I've never seen any dog act like that, ever."

They went in the kitchen and, as Evvy collapsed in a chair, Isabelle fished him out of the pen. His tongue was lolling and his sides heaving from what he'd just put himself through, so she cuddled him, calming him down, as she sat down on the floor.

"Poor Beau. What's the trouble? There now, quiet down," she said, soothing him.

Evvy gestured helplessly. "Look, Isabelle, I know he's really too young to go, but he is weaned, and I think he'd be better off. It's what he seems to want, however crazy that seems, but he's fine now. And he wouldn't have been if you hadn't showed up. You said you were ready. And I damn well know *he's* ready! What took you so long getting home? It was really something."

Isabelle flushed, not wanting to admit that she'd spent an hour or more over a hot water bottle and something to read. "I just had some shopping to do, that's all. I'm awfully sorry. But about going home—I'd be so happy if he could. I was even telling him that while we were out in back." She addressed the puppy, now curled sleepily in her lap. "Right, Beau? Guess you took me too seriously."

She turned back to Evvy. "If you're sure it's okay. I'd love to. As long as it won't hurt anything."

"It's at least better than what went on while you were gone. I'm sure it'll be fine. Have you got a crate for him?"

"No, but it'll be here Thursday, they said. I can put something together to hold us in the meantime."

Evvy nodded, "Right. Something like a big grocery box or a big, deep suitcase should do it—the zippered kind. You can line either one with old towels." She paused. "Look, I'm being kind of rude, and I'm sorry. I was sort of upset. Can I fix you a drink or anything?"

"No, don't worry about it," said Isabelle. "If we're going, we'd better go. I'll get him settled, and then have a drink at home." Again she turned to Beau. "How about it, little one?" she said. He looked at her gravely, and licked her hand again. That settled it.

She handed him to Evvy while she shouldered her bag, and then she took him back, carrying him high and close. Evvy walked them to the car and opened the door to the back deck for them.

"No, that's all right," said Isabelle. "He can ride up front with me."

"You sure? He might get in your way."

"We'll be fine. It's just a short drive, and back roads all the way." She slipped into the driver's seat, and deposited Beau beside her. She thanked Evvy and turned the ignition key, then resettled Beau, who'd begun to explore. "Now be good, and be quiet."

Evvy waved them goodbye and went back in the house. "The hell with it," she muttered. "She might not need a drink, but I certainly do." She poured herself a gin and tonic and stretched out on the sofa in the family room. Someone else would car-pool the children this afternoon. Thank God. She'd never had a worse couple of hours in her life.

Isabelle was well down Middlesex Road, past Ox Ridge, before she really noticed how well Beau was behaving—no whimpering, no jumping, no wandering, nothing. He'd settled down quietly in his seat, as though he'd done it and seen it all before, but his bright black eyes never left her.

She smiled down at him. "Well, there. Aren't you the best fellow? And isn't this a nice surprise? I'm ready for you, though. I've got food, and bones, and toys, and I'll fix you a bed. And we'll be best friends, right?" She took a hand off the wheel and touched his shoulder.

"Now what shall we do when we get home? Have a walk, I guess, and show you around. Then another walk after you've had some supper. And early to bed, since Peter's not home. Not very exciting, you say?" She was pleased with this conversation, for he seemed to be holding up his end by paying keen attention. "Right you are. Smart dog. But you're too little to stay up late, and I guess I'm too big."

The stoplight was red, and she waited to turn left. "Won't be long now," she said, patting him again. And then they were headed down Noroton Avenue.

"I sent your registration papers in this morning, so you'll have them if you want to go to dog shows when you're bigger. But that doesn't matter so much to me. I got you for you, Beau," she said, weaving around a line of cars turning into the shopping center. She did not speak again until they were turning left onto the Post Road.

"I guess I should tell you," she said then, "that my old dog died. I loved him a lot, but I'm not asking you to take his place for me. He was himself, and you're yourself. Right? But I need a friend, and so do you, so now we have each other. And I'll take good care of you, and you'll take good care of me."

And then they were down the Neck and home. She pulled the car carefully into the garage, stopped, and then carried Beau to the lawn.

"Here we are, Beau. It's home. Do you like it?" she said, putting him down. He looked back at her, waddled over to a bed of daffodils, and relieved himself. Then he turned, forepaws flat on the ground, rump high, and tail waving; he barked and leaped sideways in an invitation to play.

"Come along, around back."

He followed along, puppy style, darting around her and in front of her, zigging and zagging, sniffing everything that caught his attention, and making little forward headway. Lingering in the late afternoon sunshine, her progress thoroughly stalled, she could only laugh delightedly at his enthusiastic clowning.

"Oh, puppy, come on," she urged. "Let's go see the water, before the light goes. The water's what makes that wonderful salty smell."

Finally, he fell in beside her, caught now by the drift of salt-scented air from the Sound. Near the back garden wall, she stopped to lift him up, knowing that he could not—with his nearsighted canine eyes—see what she wanted him to. But she held him in one hand and pointed with the other, down toward the shining water that sparkled in the setting sun. "See? That's it. And tomorrow, I'm going to show you your collar and leash, and we'll walk down and see it up close. We can even play in the sand. Okay?" Snuggling him against her, she turned back toward the house.

"Come on," she said. "Let's get you some supper and a bed."

She let him down again, and he trailed her as she walked slowly, accommodating his pace, back up the lawn and through the garage to the door that led to the laundry room and the kitchen beyond. He could not make the steps, so she picked him up and didn't set him down again until they were in the kitchen.

"Now. Dinner. One scoop of dry food, one of water, one of canned. Little coat supplement. How does that suit you? I even got you some new dishes." He watched her solemnly as she got it ready, and ate eagerly once she'd set his dish on the floor. She poured herself a Scotch and water, and watched him eat.

"Good boy, Beau. Good," she said when he finished. "Now your milk, for the bones and teeth." She laughed. "Wouldn't want anything to happen to those teeth." She pierced a can of evaporated milk and poured about a third of it into the now empty bowl. He lapped up almost all of it.

"Good boy. Now we'll go outside and you

can run that off. You must be stuffed. What a hungry bear!"

She led him out through the garage, lifting him over the steps, and then going back for her drink. Sipping at it, she strolled along as he explored—bouncing, leaping, lurching, but always running back to the shelter of her feet—until it grew so dark that she was afraid of losing sight of him. "Time to go, Beau. Got to get your bed fixed. Want a ride?" She crouched down and held out her hands to him, and he came and nestled in her arms until they were in the house.

"Now, what do we do for a bed, Beau?" she asked him, setting him down in the laundry room. Her eye fell on a laundry basket; the big old-fashioned wicker kind that she'd always used had worked as a makeshift bassinet for Johnny years before, and would be just as appropriate for the puppy. She left him in the laundry room while she rummaged the upstairs linen closet for old towels. Finding enough to do the job, she piled them in her arms and went back downstairs, where she tried—against his running at her hands and feet—to get the basket lined. Finally, she finished, and put him in. Beau, obviously, took this for some new game. But once she'd filled the hot water bottle and wound the clock, and tucked them both just beneath the top layer of toweling, he was comforted by the warmth and by the ticking, and rapidly calmed down. It would be all right, she thought, to carry the whole affair into the study and put it next to her chair. Within seconds after she'd done so, Beau was sound asleep.

"Okay, Beau," she said, "now that you're fine, I'll get myself something to eat and come in here with you. Be right back."

He didn't awaken until she'd finished her light supper and washed up. This time, she took him for another brief walk and brought him right in again. She locked up and, on impulse, instead of leaving the puppy in the laundry room, she lugged him—basket and all—upstairs with her, and put the burden down beside the bed. She thought he'd be happier if he had some company.

At five-fifteen, with the light barely breaking in the east, Isabelle awoke slowly to the sound of whimpering. She'd been dreaming of Patch, and it took her a minute to orient herself, lean over the side of the bed and say, "Morning, early bird. How are you? You must need to go out."

She gave him a reassuring pat, scuffed hurriedly into a bathrobe and slippers, and carried him outside, where she placed him, wobbly legged, on the lawn. She laughed as his slightly anxious expression was replaced by a kind of bliss. "Poor puppy! You really had to go. Let me get a coat and we'll go for a little walk."

She ducked back in and grabbed her

sheepskin against the morning chill, at the same time changing her slippers for a pair of old loafers from the hall closet. When she went back outside, Beau was playing around the steps, obviously unsure of venturing off without her company. She sat down on the steps and reached out to him.

"Aren't we the pair? I haven't been up this early in a long time, and it's really a nice time of the day. Here, come and I'll give you a snuggle." She picked him up and set him on her lap, his small face inches from her own, and stroked him silently for a long moment.

"Here, I've got an idea. I'll walk with you around the property lines, to show you where they are. And then we'll have some breakfast and go to the beach." She sat him down again, and started for the wall that separated their property from the road, Beau stepping high beside her in the damp grass, and darting at the hem of the plaid bathrobe that fluttered beneath her coat.

"Now that wall," she said, pointing to it, "goes all the way around the property. Everything inside the wall is ours. And everything outside the wall is someone else's. So unless we ask people here, or friends come to see us, no one but us belongs inside the wall. And unless you're with me, you stay inside the wall. All the time."

She'd reached the wall itself and tapped on it for emphasis. Beau regarded her with an expression that represented, she thought, either grave incomprehension, or astonishment at the stream of talk. She really hadn't talked this much in years. Not just for the fun of chatting. What did it matter? There was no one to hear.

She turned right and walked to the corner, down to the back garden, across the Sound side, and back up to the garage, the puppy frisking along beside her and listening to her as she told him where the daffodils, the tulips, the roses, the grapes, and the raspberries would be in the seasons to come.

She raised the garage door. "I think that's enough for now," she said. "We both need some breakfast, and I absolutely have to have some coffee."

She got his meal ready, and fetched his basket from upstairs while he ate. When he'd finished, and had another short run, she tucked him back into the basket, stuffed and exhausted, and let him sleep while she bathed and straightened up. He was still sleeping when she came downstairs, and she smiled at the sight of him, half buried in the toweling and snoring lightly.

"Nice little fellow," she said. "And you've been so good. No accidents, no crying. Just a sweet thing." She poured herself a second cup of coffee, and sat down cross-legged next to the basket. He didn't stir.

"I'm so glad you're here, Beau," she whispered. "I'd be so lonesome without you, and I'm having such a good time." Sipping her coffee, she waited for him to wake up, not wanting to move lest she disturb him. By the time he awoke, she was stiff with sitting there, and as ready for a run as he was. As he rolled, and stretched, and shook himself into alertness, she got slowly to her feet.

"How about the beach, Beau? It looks as if it's going to rain later, but if we go now, we can certainly be home before it starts. And you can learn something about the collar and leash. I'll go get them."

She'd hung the new things from the rack in the hall, where the old ones had always hung—a light black nylon slip collar and a sturdy leather lead. She retrieved them, threw on a heavy woolen poncho that hung in the closet, and went back to the kitchen.

"Now look," she said, resuming her place by the basket, and putting the leash on the floor. "This is a slip collar." She held it up. "It works like this. You drop the collar part back through one of the metal rings, like this. Now, if you pull on the other one, the collar tightens. See?" More grave incomprehension.

"Okay," she said, laughing at her own explanation, "the part of the collar attached to the nothing-happens piece goes on top, and the metal pieces go on the right side of your neck, and the leash attaches to the makes-it-short piece." This was funny! "If that makes it all perfectly clear."

She'd even managed to confuse herself with her explanation, so it took her an extra moment to slip the collar on him correctly. At least he was sitting up by then, apparently intent on the sound of her voice and the movement of the collar in her slender hands. Finally, she had it around his neck, and snapped the leash into place.

"Triumph!" she said. "And then I pick you up and we go outside to see how the whole thing works." She held him close, and ran her cheek along this back. "Good dog," she said, "not to mention patient."

Outside, she set him down and smoothed out the lead, standing so that Beau was on her left side, more or less even with her feet. "Now. You stay on my left, and watch my left foot to see which way we're going, and try to stay even. Watch. I'll start off on my left foot." She stepped out, saying, "Beau, heel!" and the little dog followed.

"That's right. Good dog." She kept walking, slowly enough for him to keep pace, but smoothly. On the way up the driveway, he tried dashing forward, then dawdling behind, but, each time he fell out of step the collar tightened, persuading him to stay next to Isabelle and thereby to keep the collar loose and comfortable.

She continued to make a circuit of the front garden, turning right and right again, each turn tightening the collar and throwing the pup a bit off balance. By the time they were on their third time around, Beau was turning with her, scrambling at the corners, but trotting smoothly at her side on the straights. Then, and only then, did Isabelle stoop down to him, press his rump down and make him sit, and then bend to ruffle his ears and praise him lavishly.

"Okay, little one. That's your first lesson in being a civilized dog, and that's the lesson for the day. Now we can go to the beach. Okay, Beau, heel!" she said, stepping off once more with her left foot.

They walked up the road, and then down the hill toward Pear Tree beach. It was all but deserted this time of the year, and only a dozen boats rocked gently in their slips. Isabelle and Beau crossed the broad parking lot to the green clapboard shack that housed the lifeguards in summer. She sat down on the porch steps and slipped off Beau's collar and leash, stuffing them in her pants pocket.

"There you go, Beau," she said. "You're free to explore, so come on down to the water. You can do what you want, and I'll just sit on the rocks." She made her way across the sand to the breakwater, as Beau, diverted by the gentle motion of wavelets against the shore, jogged close to the waterline. Unlike Patch, who even as a pup would plunge happily into the coldest water in quest of anything that looked worth retrieving, Beau seemed to avoid getting wet, and wandered happily along the broad, firm band of sand left by the outgoing tide. He trotted out perhaps thirty feet from her, scampered back, then ventured a bit farther and came back again. Then he discovered the softer sand farther up the beach. It seemed to offer him the perfect medium for digging, and, tail wagging gaily, he applied himself earnestly to making a puppy-sized ditch.

Isabelle, bemused, watched him so intently that she failed to hear the sound of footsteps approaching from the other side of the breakwater, and jumped when the man addressed her.

"Morning, ma'am. Haven't seen you down here for a while."

It was The Old Man, as she thought of him, the gray-bearded fellow who lived God alone knew where, and who toured the town aimlessly, endlessly, on his bicycle. She knew little about him, except that in some way he was her friend—one of the few people she talked with regularly. It didn't matter to her that he was somewhat wild-eyed. He was not any crazier than anyone else she knew, she was sure of that. And he did love dogs.

"Morning," she said. "You startled me. It's nice to see you. I haven't been down in several days."

"Where's the old pup?" he said. "I've got his bone here."

She shook her head. "He's gone. He'd been sick, you know. He was awfully old, and I had to have him put down. Up there's my new puppy, Beau." She pointed to him, but he was an indistinguishable black something burrowing in the loose sand.

"I'm awful sorry. He was a nice old pooch, ma'am, awful nice." He squinted up the beach, clambered over the breakwater, and sat down next to her.

"Name's Beau, huh? Labrador?"

"No," she said. "Belgian shepherd. He's not even six weeks old."

"Mind if I pick him up and have a look?"

"Of course I don't. Wait a minute. I'll call him."

She got up and cupped her hands into a megaphone. "Beau, come on. Beau!" He left off his digging and trotted toward her. "There's someone here who wants to meet you. Come be introduced. He's a friend. It's okay," she said.

She sat down with the pup, and gently brushed the sand from his coat before handing him to the old man, who cupped him carefully in enormous, weather-beaten hands. "This is Beau," she said apologetically, "but you know, I don't even know your name. Mine's Isabelle Buckingham."

"Mine's Roberts, ma'am, Captain Amos Roberts. Glad to make your acquaintance. Now let's see this fellow. Lord! Looks like he isn't going to be a little fella for long. Quite a set of feet he's got there. Some kind of police dog, wouldn't you say? Bound to be right smart if he is." He hugged Beau to him with his right arm, and rummaged his pockets with his left hand.

"Now there, pup," he said, "I carry biscuits around for my pals, but I don't think I got one your size." He pulled a big one from the depths of his capacious pockets and flourished it. Still holding Beau, he sank to his knees, let the puppy down, and handed the biscuit to Isabelle as if it were a valuable object.

"You break that up a bit and give him some for lunch, Mrs. B. It's good for him." He turned to Beau with a look of mock sternness. "And you, pup, you got a nice missy there. She'll take good care of you, and you watch out for her."

He staggered to his feet and tipped his battered cap with one hand. "Mrs. B. Pup. Another time. Good day to you both." He had turned and begun to walk stiffly away when Isabelle called to him.

"Captain Roberts. Wait. My house is just up the road, and I'd be pleased if you'd come have some coffee and maybe a bite of lunch with us. It's going to rain soon, and I've got to get him back for his lunch and a rest anyway. Would you?"

The old fellow seemed pleased to be asked. "You sure?" he said. When she nodded in affirmation, he smiled broadly. "Been a long time since anybody asked me out, ma'am, you can be sure of that. Be delighted."

So she tucked a sleepy Beau into a sling made from her poncho, and walked up the hill slowly, with Captain Roberts pushing his bicycle silently alongside. They reached the house just ahead of the scudding clouds and the first raindrops. She tucked Beau into his basket, and threw together some tuna fish sandwiches and tea, which Roberts tackled as if he hadn't eaten in days. Finally, after seconds, he sat back, wiped his mouth and beard, and said, "I've heard tell you're a fine cook, Mrs. B., but I can't vouch for that. But I will say, you make a mean sandwich. Those were fine."

She smiled across the table at him. "Heard tell?" she said.

"Yes, ma'am. My daughter-in-law don't cook worth shit, if you'll pardon the expression, and my boy much admires your cooking."

She couldn't understand what he was talking about for a minute and her brain raced to catch up. Could he mean Bob Roberts? Was this Bob's father, and Zizi's father-in-law? She tried not to gape. "Bob and Zizi, you mean?" she said.

"Why naturally," he answered, as though there were something that made particular sense about that, "though you ain't the least likely to get them to own up to that. Put on too many airs, those two. Here I am, an old tug captain. And her old man was nothing but a goddamned Neapolitan stonemason." He gave a whinny of disapproval, and shook his head.

"Don't matter to me that much, you understand. Just ranks a fellow a bit, not to be acknowledged at all. That's what happens when you scrimp and save up and send kids to college and that. They go beyond you, sort of, and don't want to come back."

Somewhere outside of herself, she was saying, "Well, I can certainly understand how you feel about that, Captain Roberts, and I must admit I'm kind of surprised that Bob and Zizi would act that way. You seem like a perfectly presentable relative to me, and we'd be happy, Beau and I, to adopt you any time. Any time at all." She shot him what she hoped was her brightest, sunniest, most unfazeable smile, and stood up.

After Roberts had gone, she tucked Beau—basket and all—into the car, and went up to town to do her errands. It wasn't until midafternoon that she thought to call Evvy. She wanted to tell her how good he'd been, how well it had gone. But Evvy was busy, polite but busy, and asked if she could return the call later. By six, when the rain had let up, and she was sure that Evvy wasn't going to call back, Isabelle took Beau out in the fading light. Intent on enjoying a tour of the garden with her pup, she heard the telephone ringing.

"To hell with it, Beau," she said, and would not go in to answer it—stood, instead, with a drink in her hand, watching Beau protectively, and counting the rings until the sound ceased.

After supper, working on her needlepoint, with Beau in his basket at her feet, she was startled by the telephone. Certain it would be Evvy, she was surprised to hear Peter's voice on the other end of the line.

"Oh. Hi, dear." Her voice sounded strange, even to her.

"What's the matter?" he said. "I tried to reach you earlier, and now you sound funny."

"Nothing. It's just that I'd forgotten that it was Tuesday, and that you'd be calling. I thought it must be Evvy."

He laughed. "With the bedtime report?" he asked.

"What?"

"The bedtime report. On Beau."

"No. No, he's home already. I brought him home yesterday. I got all his stuff. He wanted..." She stopped, afraid it sounded crazy. She could explain it later.

"But, Isabelle, he's barely six weeks old. He's not ready to come home."

"Listen. Evvy said he was, and he's just fine. It's all right with Rog, too. Now, how's the trip?"

She could almost hear him shrug.

"Trip's all right. That hand hurts like hell, though. I forgot to ask you when I left, though. Do you need any money? How much did all this dog stuff set you back?"

"I'm okay. It was about two hundred for Beau and another hundred for supplies."

"Three hundred bucks! I'm not criticizing, but don't you think that's a bit much?"

"Peter, please. You give me a set sum every month. Isn't it up to me how I spend it?"

"I guess so. Do what you want. I'll see you Friday, all right? I'll be through Thursday at noon, and I'll take the rest of the day, spend the night, and come up on a flight that will let me go straight to the office. Then I'll knock off a little early Friday afternoon," he said. "It's too nice down here not to enjoy it a little, and I've been working pretty steadily. Okay with you?"

"That's fine, Peter. It sounds really pleasant. But call me when you get to the office on Friday."

"I sure will, honey. I was going to ask you to come down and join me—maybe even spend the weekend. But I guess you wouldn't be able to now, right?"

"I guess not, but have a good time," she said, knowing full well that no invitation would have been forthcoming if she'd actually been able to take him up on it. "See you then, dear. Good night."

"Good night, darling," said Peter. He hung up the telephone, stepped out of the phone booth, and shouldered his way back to the bar. A tanned and handsome blonde was waiting for him, and he put a proprietary arm around her shoulder. "Okay, Sally. I've had a long working day, and you've run me all over the courts, and I've had one drink over my usual two. I'll follow where you lead, if you'll steer me to a good restaurant and be my guest."

She laughed up at him, as though he'd said something hugely witty. "Why thank you," she said. "That would be great, and I know the nicest place there is."

8

On Friday evening, when Peter let himself in, Isabelle was in the study, Beau in the laundry basket at her feet. Peter hadn't managed to make it home early; it was his usual hour, a bit after seven, and he was wearing an unwieldy bandage on his right hand. "What's the matter?" said Isabelle.

"It infected," he said shortly, not bothering with even a perfunctory kiss, and instead making straight for the Scotch bottle. "I had to see a doctor in Atlanta and have it opened up and cauterized. Hurts like hell." Plainly, he was tired, and didn't feel like talking. He didn't feel like eating, either, and waved aside supper, instead pouring himself a third drink. When he went to pat Beau, the little dog shrank away from him, seeming to sense his mood.

Peter got up, wearily. "Guess I'll get some crackers and cheese," he said, heading for the kitchen. Surveying the cupboards, he noticed, out of the corner of his eye, that there was a new dog crate abandoned in the laundry room. It struck him that there were no newspapers on the floor, and there seemed to him to be something odd about that. He fixed his crackers, and carried them back to the study.

"Isabelle," he said, "what about the papers?"

"Oh, I got them from Evvy and sent them to the AKC. I chose Beaumont's Black Bandit. Do you like it?"

"I didn't mean registration papers," he said. "Newspapers. For the floor."

"Oh, he doesn't need them. He's on this new method—three meals at regular hours, water when he wants it, and a walk after each meal and first thing in the morning. Last thing at night, too. It works, too. Not a single mistake so far."

"That's nice. And is he sleeping in the laundry room?"

She'd have to be careful with this. She paused. "Well, no, not really, not yet. I've been taking his basket upstairs with me after his last walk, and having it next to the bed. That way, he doesn't cry at all, and everyone sleeps better."

Peter took a long, silent swig of his drink, annoyance visible in every line of the gesture. "I'd rather not have him there," he said.

Two could play that game. Isabelle went to the desk, found and lit a cigarette—an old one, stale and harsh, but it would do for effect. She looked at him, eyebrows raised.

"Really, Peter? It seems to me that you're not here all that much. I always am, and there's nothing the matter with it. We'll all sleep better if he stays upstairs, so that's where he's staying."

Something must have disturbed Beau just then, for he raised his head sharply, and looked from Peter to Isabelle and back again, his ears pricked, as though listening to something of intense interest.

"I'll be home all next week..." he began. But his protest faded. *Christ, I'm being ridiculous,* he thought, recalling the fan of tawny hair and the flash of green eyes. *Why not let her have her way? What in hell could the dog disturb that isn't disturbed already?*

"Okay, Isabelle," he said. "It's your problem if he ruins the rug. Mind some music?"

"No, of course not. Go ahead." Her point made, she snuffed out the cigarette.

He considered the row of tapes, selected one, and set it on the player. A Bach quartet flooded the room, as Peter moved to place the frame in front of her chair.

"Don't bother, dear," she said. "I don't feel like it tonight. I'll just sit down on the floor with the puppy and read for a while before I take him out. We've had a busy day."

With that, she slid down beside the basket and ran her hand lightly down Beau's back. They settled into silence, save for the music. When the tape ran out, Peter put another on, but Isabelle and Beau got up. She took him outside and carried his basket upstairs before returning to collect him again. With Beau in her arms, she stood in the door of the study.

"Good night, dear. I guess you're going to wait for the tape to finish?"

He nodded. "I'll be up soon."

On Saturday, Peter was jolted awake by the pup's whimpering, by the feel and sound of Isabelle slipping out of bed and into her robe and slippers to take Beau out. Rolling over to check the clock, he groaned at the hour. Five-thirty. Maybe he could go back to sleep. He huddled down, but he could not shut off the soft morning sounds—doors being opened and shut, the murmur of Isabelle talking to Beau, cupboards opening and closing, the muffled clatter of pots and dishes. He could not sleep, and knew that he would spend the rest of the day with fatigue eating at the edges of his temper, dulling his reflexes and his judgment.

Finally he threw the covers back. "Well, dammit, it's your fault that she got the pup. At least he'll grow out of it," he muttered, as he swung his feet around. He felt lousy—his hand sore, his tongue fuzzy from the Scotch the night before. A shower would help set him up, he felt, and he ran a long one—warm, hot, warm, cool, cold, and finally cold enough to make his teeth rattle. Afterward, he toweled himself off, shaved carefully, and dressed, slamming doors and drawers to make audible his annoyance at being awakened so early. "Shit!" he said, staring angrily at the contents of his closet. "I'm not even going to be able to play today."

By the time he got downstairs, Beau had had his breakfast and his run, and had collapsed in the corner by Isabelle's chair. Peter's coffee and orange juice were at his place, and Isabelle was making waffles—obviously a peace offering to her disgruntled husband. She tried, gently, to ask why he hadn't been able to go back to sleep, but he only glared at her. Breakfast was all but silent until Peter leaned back in his chair.

"Does he seem to have established five-thirty as his regular rising hour? If that's the case, I wonder why you didn't go at this thing straightforwardly, and simply buy a rooster." He laughed without humor at his joke, and did not notice that Beau had raised his head sharply, and was staring at him.

Isabelle was truly apologetic. "So far," she said, "but he's awfully young yet. He'll grow out of it, he really will. And it's better than having him keep us awake all night with crying. I don't mind getting up, really; it's a nice hour to be out. But you do, so we'll try to be quieter."

"I'd appreciate it," he said shortly.

She looked miserable. *Serves her right,* he thought, pleased to see her as uncomfortable as he was.

"Peter, I'm sorry. Maybe you'd like me to sleep in Anne's room for a while, so you won't be disturbed. I know the meetings next week are important, and I know you need your rest." Her suggestion was offhand, but his reply was short and sarcastic.

"Now there's a real suggestion. Thank you so much."

After a second cup of coffee and a lapse back into silence, he said that he'd go up and get a paper, go by the courts to tell Charlie that he wouldn't be able to play, and then take himself for a drive. With a meaningless stab at a goodbye kiss, he was gone. When he was out the door, Isabelle fetched Beau's basket from upstairs, put him in it, and got herself some more coffee and a cigarette. She lit it, dragged deeply, and laughed ruefully.

"Beau," she said, "we have offended our lord and master with our peasant habits. How about that? It's time somebody did, my friend, but don't quote me. Peter's had it all his own way for years, you know. That's true."

She wasn't laughing now. Her voice was clouding with tears.

"All these years, Beau. I did things for the

kids and I did things for Peter. And now they don't need me anymore, not really. Now I need them sometimes, and they're all somewhere else, with people who interest them more than I do. Because, right now, I'm just not very interesting. I garden, and I keep house, and I do needlework, and I read. My best friend died five years ago, and I'm just not very good at meeting people. So aside from being reasonably well educated, I have done not one single interesting or individual thing in my whole adult life." She thought about that for a moment before she went on. It seemed to her to be all too true.

"Not one," she said finally. "I'm not a kid anymore, Beau, and I can't start over, so I just go on with it, the best way I know how. I had Patch, you know—I told you about that—and he was my only real company for a while. I used to talk to him, too. It isn't that I'm recently crazy or anything." She laughed a little at that.

"Okay, Beau. There's no point in being morbid. What is, is. But at the moment, you're all I've got—really got—and I'm all you've got. So let's discreetly pretend that I'm not really so lonesome that the only people I can talk to are a puppy and a crazy old man. Why don't the two of us, maybe with the help of the crazy old man, go out and do something that everyone will notice? How would that be?"

He looked sympathetic to that idea. She had

to say that. He seemed to be hanging on every word she said.

"I know you're loving, Beau, and I'll just bet you're smart, too. Let's try these obedience things, and bring home lots of prizes. You look as if you think that's a good idea. Perfect. Now, I'll do the housework, and then we'll go down to the beach for a lesson and see if we can find Captain Roberts. I bet he'd love it. He's lonesome, too. We'll do fifteen minutes a day, and see how it goes." She finished off by giving him an extra cuddle, and then, cheered by her own resolve, hastened to finish the housework so she could get down to the beach.

As it turned out, Captain Roberts was delighted with the idea. "Never heard of it," he said, "but I will say it makes a whole hell of a lot more sense than giving out prizes for looking good, you'll forgive my language, ma'am. Be glad to help, any old how. Sure would."

So it was settled. Through the spring, as Beau grew through puppyhood and lanky adolescence, as his ears straightened to their most alert and wolflike erectness, as his coat filled out and feathered on belly and legs and tail, they worked at it, down at the beach. Isabelle and Captain Roberts passed back and forth a copy of a fat tome called *Toward the Ph.D. for Dogs* until it grew tattered. They studied each lesson solemnly, until they had it memorized, and then practiced over and over.

Beau never seemed to grow tired of it, and he learned quickly, mastering the lessons as fast as they could give them. By the time the summer season opened, and the beach was barred to dogs for the weeks until Labor Day, they'd mastered a good part of the book. True, the first lessons were simple, and Beau's achievements, however large they seemed to Isabelle and Captain Roberts, were small and pale beside those of Brummel and Serena. First it was heeling, with Isabelle going in a straight line, then through right turns, then through left turns, and finally through figure eights. This Beau mastered in a week, through every possible change of pace, always sitting—first with a push, then on his own—the moment Isabelle came to a halt. This part was harder, for his fat puppy belly got in the way of his sitting straight, but soon enough he had the hang of doing it without leaning up against her. He got the idea of correction quickly, too, and learned to respond immediately to the slightest tug on his lead.

Finally, the lesson complete, Roberts supervised a final test of heeling skills. Isabelle started off with the one command, "Beau, heel!" and then—dawdling, marching, pacing, running—went through a mad series of turns with Beau keeping exactly even with her left knee throughout. When it was over, and Beau sat square and straight at her side, she said, "Okay, Beau!" slipped his collar off, and tussled with him, laughing delightedly. "We done it, Mrs. B. Now what's next?" said Roberts, as they walked up the hill toward the house.

Next was heeling off leash, which came easy. Then the sit-stay and the down-stay, each at longer distances and longer times, until Beau was responding perfectly to both commands. Then, teaching him to finish up, she taught him to respond to "Beau, finish!" so that he'd come straight, turn himself around, and sit at her left side. Each lesson ended with lavish praise and patting from both her and Roberts, and then they would remove his slip collar—his working clothes— and take turns brushing him until he glistened. When the session had ended she'd fix some lunch for Roberts and herself, while Beau snoozed under the kitchen table. After Roberts left, Isabelle and Beau would go about their errands, and over that spring and into the summer—by which time they had switched the training sessions from the beach to Isabelle's garden—the slight blonde woman and her handsome black puppy became a familiar sight on the streets and in the shops in Darien, and even in Stamford. He was permitted in Bloomingdale's, and in Lord & Taylor. Only the supermarket barred him, and there Isabelle could leave him with a "Beau, down," for as long as a half hour, despite the pats of children and the stares of strangers.

Even Peter was reasonably impressed. And

pleased, too. It was heartening to see Isabelle really interested in something, and it eased the pressure on him somewhat. Not that he liked the idea of her hanging around with someone as downright peculiar as Amos Roberts. But what the hell? He was Bob's father, wasn't he? All that he really cared about was that Isabelle, for the first time in years, seemed both busy and cheerful, full of what she and Beau were up to, full of the details.

And if he found the details less than fascinating, it made him proud to see how much Beau was coming to resemble Brummel in both appearance and style. There were times, to be sure, when Isabelle's accounts of the week's progress wore on too long, and baffled him with intricacies that he couldn't appreciate. And if, from time to time, he felt a bit left out, that was all right, too.

The only thing that bothered him, though he seldom thought about it, was that Beau ignored him almost entirely. Where Patch had been wonderfully, indiscriminately affectionate, and very much a family dog, Beau was Isabelle's—solely, entirely, worshipfully. Unless told to do otherwise, he followed her everywhere. And she talked to him all the time, even when Peter was there. He knew she must make even more of a habit of that in his absence.

In fact, he was entirely out of it until Isabelle asked him, one Friday evening, to construct a pulley rig to help with the final lesson required for the Companion Dog trials, the recall. She didn't think she'd have trouble with it, she told him. Beau already answered to his name. But it was essential that he learn to come in straight and true to sit right in front of her, within arm's reach, and the pulley rig would help with that. Glad, at last, to be included, Peter stopped off at the hardware store on his way back from tennis the next afternoon, and purchased the requisite lengths of rope and the pulleys. In twenty minutes, he had the rig put together. And by the next Saturday, Beau had mastered it.

The next lesson, since he was already heeling perfectly without the lead as well as with it, was to stand for examination. For this Isabelle needed a stranger, and called Evvy, who admiringly pronounced Beau perfect after two twenty-minute sessions. She couldn't have done better with a dog herself, she said, with just a tinge of envy. Isabelle thought that high praise indeed, and was delighted to take Evvy up on her offer to practice together for the next few weeks, refining the events under simulated show conditions with the Hutchinsons' dogs. This was the final polish that should make Beau a winner.

She was as excited as a child when she told Captain Roberts about the sessions, sure that he'd join her for them, but he declined, saying, "Nope, Mrs. B. Just not much of a one for folks, I guess." But he cheerfully checked the dog show schedule for her, and selected three New England shows scheduled close together in late July. These would be their goal—three shows in four days, scores of 170 or better in each, and the C.D. degree as fast and "fussless," as he called it, as possible.

When she spoke to Evvy about it, it turned out that the Hutchinsons would be showing at the same three shows, not in the novice A that would be Beau's class, but in the more advanced open category. They, veterans of the wars between motel keepers and dog owners, would made the reservations and help her out. The plans were to return on Saturday night, and Peter agreed to fend for himself in the couple of days she'd be gone. Isabelle, for her part, promised to call Amos Roberts each night with news of how she'd done. Roberts helped her pack the car that Wednesday morning, answering her nervous questions and doing his best to reassure her that Beau would triumph. Sure, it was hot, but it wouldn't bother Beau. Didn't matter if he was so young; at six months, he could stand up against the best of them. He'd be fine.

And he was fine. He certainly was. In the first show, he scored 198½, highest in his class for a blue ribbon and a little trophy. The second day, a 195 and a red ribbon. And on Saturday, a 199 to take the class, a blue ribbon, his degree, and a special award. Barely able to contain herself, she called Peter to tell him she was starting home, and Amos Roberts to thank him for all the help that had made it possible. "Knew you'd do it, Mrs. B. See you for lunch Monday, like always, but we ought to give the pup a couple of days off." Good thought, that, she felt, as she set out for home. All the hard work had paid off, and they deserved the rest. On the way home, she stopped and picked up three steaks; whatever Peter might think of the extravagance, she felt that Beau had earned his. But Peter was in an indulgent mood, and even broke out a fine bottle of Chateauneuf du Pape for the celebration.

"Well, Isabelle, what now?" he said, over a late brandy, gesturing toward her in a way that included the dog sleeping soundly across her feet. "I guess you got what you set out for."

"But I can't see stopping there, can you, Peter?" she asked, genuinely surprised by the idea. He couldn't mean it. "He's so good at it, and I thought I'd keep showing him around in graduate novice while I get him ready for the open classes. It won't take long, I'm sure." She beamed with pride. "I'm just the handler, you know. Beau's the winner. You really should have seen him. He was terrific. Even Evvy said she'd never seen a dog do this well this young."

Not that it made any sense to him, but it seemed to mean so much to her. "I'm proud of you both, Isabelle," said Peter, "and if you want to go on with it, I'm with you. Within reason, of course. You seem to be having a good time with it, and I guess you're finally glad that we talked you into getting him after all."

"Oh, but Peter," she said rubbing Beau's back with one bare foot, "you didn't talk me into it. He did."

The following Saturday, Isabelle asked Peter if he'd construct a hurdle, similar to a regulation track hurdle, to train Beau for returns and retrieves over a jump. She had the measurements, and a rough drawing that Captain Roberts had done to guide him, and gave them to him over breakfast. "Fine," he said. "Glad to do it." But privately he thought it an imposition.

"Last month the goddamn pulley, and now this frigging thing," he said to himself on his way back from the hardware store. "I'll say this for that rotten dog: at least he seems to know who's boss around there." Without enthusiasm, he spent the afternoon marking the pieces and rough-cutting them. Then, early Sunday, he began the construction, working slowly in the warm August sunshine, taking special care that the work should be perfectly done. First, he cut and sanded the crosspieces, and then he measured and routed the uprights and the bases. By the time he was ready to peg the pieces together, Isabelle had let Beau out for a run in the garden.

Beau had never left the property unbidden,

never wandered. Peter had grown accustomed to it, and it no longer struck him as remarkable in any way. It was simply convenient that they never had to keep an eye on him. He had also resigned himself to the fact that Beau always ignored him, never offered his head for stroking, never wanted to play with him.

Not that Beau wouldn't play with Isabelle. He'd play for hours with her, like a puppy. He'd even learned to snatch a flying Frisbee from the air and bring it back to her. Not like Patch, not at all. What did it matter? Peter guessed it didn't, not really. He simply didn't much like this dog. There was something intimidating about the animal, about the way a rather wolfish look combined with an aloof manner to put him off.

Now, however, Beau stood but a few inches away, looking at the pieces of the jump with an expression that, on a human face, Peter would have called interest, even curiosity. There was something eager about him—something Peter had never seen in him unless Isabelle was nearby. But since the work was, at the best of it, fairly slow going, Beau soon settled down, head on paws, to watch. As the job wore on, Peter began to feel somewhat foolish under that steady gaze. He began to understand why Isabelle so often talked to Beau. As he worked toward completing the hurdle, he was moved by an almost irresistible compulsion to speak.

He cleared his throat, and addressed the

dog in a voice that might otherwise have been reserved for dressing down an errant child or an out-of-line subordinate. "See here, young fellow. This is for you. You're going to learn to jump over it, and retrieve dumbbells and things like that. It's part of the next degree. You learn to do this, and some other stuff, and there'll be more silver and more ribbons and more steaks for dinner." He tapped the last board into place, and checked the hurdle for balance and stability. "What do you think?"

Moving the thing to a level place on the lawn, he called Isabelle to have a look. As he did so, Beau rose from his place, stretched to and fro, and strolled over, wagging his tail, to sniff the hurdle. Peter stopped to watch him, and saw for the first time how truly beautiful he was—perfectly proportioned, beautifully groomed, and so obviously intelligent. He couldn't love him, but he could admire him. Caught up as he was in this thought, he was totally unprepared for what happened next for, as he watched, Beau backed off a few steps, placed himself square to the jump, and then, with a running start, cleared the hurdle. In an instant, before Peter could recover from the initial surprise, he lined himself up once again, and jumped it a second time from the opposite direction.

Startled, Peter could hardly believe what he'd just seen. He called Beau to him, uncertain that he would come, but Beau strolled over until he stood just out of reach.

He looked up at Peter with an expression that Peter could not read. He did not seem to want approval; in fact, he backed off when Peter reached out to stroke his silky head. It was only late that night that Peter realized where he'd seen that look before—on the face of one of his up-and-coming young staffers, a man that he knew was after his job. It was a challenge. And he didn't like it at all.

9

At first, it did not occur to Isabelle that there was anything so remarkable in what Beau had done. To her, he was simply the brightest, most responsive, most affectionate dog that had ever been. But on Monday, when she told Captain Roberts about the incident, he said something that somehow stuck. "Well, Mrs. B., your old Beau's the smartest goddamn dog I ever saw, no holds barred, you'll pardon my language. Wouldn't much surprise me if he could read minds or the *New York Times*, it came to that." he said. "But we got to teach him this other stuff, so we'd best get on it."

"This other stuff" was the remaining series

of exercises for the C.D.X. degree. Added to the heeling exercises and the long sit and long down would be four more maneuvers—retrieving a wooden dumbbell on the flat and over the hurdle, clearing a broad jump obstacle, and dropping flat on recall.

That morning, they worked with the dumbbell and the commands, "Take it," "Hold it," and "Out." Once he'd gotten the hang of them, Isabelle tossed the dumbbell on the flat, signaling him to stay beside her until she ordered, "Take it!" At this, he'd run for it, pick it up, and bring it back, stopping right in front of her, and sitting as he did so. In two twenty-minute sessions, Beau had this part down pat.

The next day, he mastered the retrieves over the hurdle, as she had somehow known he would. Next would come what Isabelle was sure would be the hardest exercise, the broad jump and the drop on recall. After lunch, lingering on the lawn over a last glass of iced tea, she said as much to Captain Roberts. "I think we can get him to do the broad jump, Captain, but I don't even understand the instructions for that drop on recall, do you?"

"Can't say I do, ma'am, but you can be sure Beau will. Understands everything. Don't really have to teach him—just have to show him what you want and he'll do it. Look what he did with that hurdle for Mr. B. over the weekend. Just caught the idea of it right away, you know. Uncanny smart he is. Met lots of folks dumber than him in my day, I surely have." He chortled at that, and she laughed with him.

"Tell you what," he said. "You keep working him on the other stuff, but if you'll pick up some boards at the hardware, I can put that broad jump stuff together. How'd that be? But for the moment, I'd best be on my way. See you tomorrow." He rose, gave Beau a final pat, and trudged toward his bicycle, which, lacking a kickstand, he'd propped against the side of the garage. At the top of the drive, he turned and waved, and, as Isabelle responded in kind, she was suddenly swept by a wave of fondness for the old man, by gratitude for his company and his willingness to share her enthusiasm.

Beau lay down beside her, and she leaned over to tell him what a fine dog he was. "I wonder, Beau, if you really do know what we want. Maybe we should try to find out, hmmm? Let's see." She stroked him for a moment, then stood up and, ordering him to stay, walked as far away as she could across the lawn before she turned back to face him. "Beau, come!" she called. He scrambled to his feet and launched himself toward her. When he was halfway there, she gave him the hand signal to drop; it was the lesson she felt least certain he would master, and thereby a good test of his abilities. Immediately, though he'd been running full tilt toward her, he dropped to the ground. Oddly, she was not really surprised, and immediately gave him the command to continue to come. He trotted up to her, finished properly, and accepted her praise with grave equanimity. "Good, Beau. Good! What a smart dog you are!" she said, hugging his great head to her.

She sat back again, trying to think of some other experiment. She noticed a rake propped against the wall, where she'd been clearing some weeds. She walked over and picked it up, hefting it to find where she could hold it comfortably by the wrong end. Feeling silly enough that she was glad there was no one to watch her, she swung the stout handle slightly downward. "Okay, Beau," she said, "hit it as hard as you can!" With a snarl, he launched himself at the rake handle, sinking his teeth into it and throwing all his weight against it. The next thing Isabelle knew, her feet had gone out from under her, and she was sitting breathlessly on the ground, Beau whimpering beside her.

She laughed, and patted him to let him know he'd done nothing wrong. "But I'm not sure," she added, "that this is anything to fool around with. I think we'd better go back to doing things the conventional way." She stood up and rubbed her bottom, shaking her head.

During the week, Captain Roberts constructed the broad jump, and they mastered the last lessons for the C.D.X. tests. After several more days of practice, Isabelle called

Evvy Hutchinson, since she'd once again reached the point where Beau's training would benefit by being with other dogs and having the distractions that would simulate a show situation.

Evvy was astonished. "But, Isabelle," she said, "you just can't be ready. You just picked up the C.D. a month ago, and the C.D.X. is much harder."

"I'd have thought it would be, too, but you'd be surprised at how quickly he's taken to it. If you'll be home in the morning, I'll come by and show you. Or maybe you'd like to bring the dogs down and have lunch and do the exercises here."

"I'd love it," said Evvy. "I'm sick of the house, and sick of the kids. I always am by August anyway. I'll be down around eleven, and we can work with the dogs and then have lunch, okay?"

"Perfect," Isabelle replied, smiling to herself in anticipation. She just wished Captain Roberts would come and have his share of the credit. But he wouldn't.

"See you then. And thanks, Isabelle."

If Evvy had had doubts, watching Beau in the simulated show ring swept them away. Acting as judge, she cued Isabelle with the order of the exercises, as they would occur in competition. She'd brought along worksheets, and scored him as objectively as she could.

"Lord, Isabelle," she said as she totaled the

points, "I just can't believe this. How old is he? Seven months, almost? And he's definitely ready to go. How'd you do it?"

Isabelle hesitated. There were some things she wasn't going to talk about, not to Evvy, not to anyone. "Well, I'm not quite sure. I followed the book, as best I could. And old Captain Roberts helped a lot. Even Peter helped a little. But as far as I can tell, it's that he has a lot of natural ability for this sort of thing, and sort of understands what you want him to do." She wondered if she should tell Evvy about how he'd jumped the hurdle both ways the minute Peter finished making it. Somehow, it didn't seem like a good idea.

"I suppose you're right," said Evvy. "But I'm sorry now that we didn't keep him. Tom is going to pass out when I tell him this. Maybe I can mollify him if you'll let us have first pick when you breed him. The score, as I figure it, is 198."

Isabelle, by now sitting on the lawn with her arms around Beau's neck, grinned. "First pick? Why not? Who else would I give it to?" And rising to her feet, she led the way to lunch.

They left Beau and Brummel and Serena in the yard, chasing each other happily, romping over the jumps, as they adjourned for salads and iced tea.

Evvy, her dishes pushed aside, offered Isabelle a cigarette and lit it. "Okay, now I want you to tell me how you really did do it.

Your secret's safe, I promise. Come on," she coaxed.

Isabelle assumed an air of bewilderment. "But I don't know. I just show him what to do and that's pretty much the end of it. Sometimes I don't even have to show him." She paused for a minute. It would be such fun just to tell Evvy about the hurdle. She'd do it. "Why, when Peter built the hurdle a couple of weeks back, when he finished it, Beau just walked over to it, sniffed it a little, and then jumped it both ways."

Evvy exhaled, long and slow, a whistling sound. "Weird," she said. "That's just weird."

"No, I don't think so," said Isabelle. "Not at all. He could see what it was for. And, after that, the broad jump was easy, and so was that drop on recall."

"Easy? The drop on recall? For my money, there's just nothing harder than that." Evvy shook her head. She smoked in silence for a moment before continuing, and when she did, she seemed to have chosen her words with extraordinary care.

"Well, you two had something special between you from the start. Remember how he insisted on coming home with you? But if it pays off in the ring," and here she smiled broadly, with a sense of having something to smile about, "I'm damned well going to take all the credit I can for having bred him. I'll just stand back and smile and raise the prices on future litters. Keep that a secret, okay? I'll keep yours, if you'll keep mine."

Together they cleared the dishes from the table, and made out entry forms for the Ox Ridge Kennel Club show, scheduled near the end of September, and for two other shows taking place around the same time and within easy driving distance. "I think he'll make that degree, with no question about it," said Evvy, as they tucked their forms and checks into envelopes.

"I hope so," said Isabelle, "but I do want you to know that there's no secret, and I think it is in the breeding. He's just awfully smart and awfully willing. I wouldn't sell him for anything, and I think you're justified in charging for your pups. I really mean that. Now, let's get some more iced tea and go see the dogs."

It was hot out, and breathlessly humid, as they carried their iced tea out under the trees. Even the dogs, frisking around their heels, seemed to have lost their bounce. "You're lucky," Evvy was saying, "to have old Roberts to help. I've got Tom, of course, but Peter doesn't really seem to be into it, does he?"

They settled down on the lawn, and Isabelle sighed. She hadn't really thought much about Peter lately, so involved had she been with other things. "The way he travels," she said, "he just doesn't have time. He's helped on the weekends a little, and he's always hearing about it, of course. But aside from the business, his main interest is the tennis. He plays every weekend—always has."

"I've heard he's terrific," said Evvy, sipping her tea. "So many people have taken it up in the last few years, but it never was my sport."

"Oh, Peter's been playing since he was a little kid. He hates the story, so I never tell it, but I guess I can tell you how it came about. When his parents got married, right after the First World War, his father bought an enormous turn-of-the-century family house in Brookline. I guess there were plans for lots of other little Buckinghams, but when Peter was two, his father died. He was in ship chandlery, down by the docks, and there was a strike on the streetcars. Well, you know Bostonians. The day it started, he walked all the way home in a rainstorm, and three days later he was gone."

Evvy seemed sympathetic enough to let her continue.

"That was early in the twenties," she went on, "and times were good. His mother turned to the business and, with the help of the staff, actually ran it for several years. But the crash wiped it out, and there they were—still in this enormous house. It was all paid for, and the taxes were so low that they literally couldn't afford to move out. Mrs. Buckingham just closed the top of the house, and she and Peter moved into the kitchen, pantry, and dining room. They only opened up the parlors when they had company." She stopped, remembering how angry he'd been when she suggested selling this house.

"Anyway, even as a child, he seems to have been one of those people who was born responsible. Since he was the male of the family, if not the man, he started working after school at anything he could find—paper routes, mowing lawns, cleaning basements, anything a youngster could do. The old man next door, Mr. Trilling, had a tennis court that he wanted mowed twice a week, and Peter got the job. After he had finished with the work, I guess, he'd sneak back and fool around with a discarded racket and spent balls. So old man Trilling started to teach him when he was seven or eight, really drilling him, and he's been at it ever since. He's won all kinds of amateur titles, but he keeps his trophies in his office, though of course there aren't so many recent ones."

She leaned back, thinking of that hot summer sun, and of that small, gritty, unknown child who'd pushed that heavy lawnmower. "It means so much to him," she continued. "When things were tight, he didn't have much, but people asked him everywhere because he could play so well. He could get teaching or coaching jobs in the summer, and things like that. Even now, you'd be surprised how many doors it opens for him in business, you really would be. So it isn't that he doesn't like Beau. I know he'll come to Ox Ridge and any other local shows. He's not really interested, that's all."

The shadows were lengthening across the lawn, and a thunderstorm was blowing up from the west. They picked up their glasses and said their goodbyes. Isabelle and Beau watched as Evvy backed her battered blue station wagon out of the drive. And when it was out of sight, she sat down and hugged Beau's neck. "We're showing them, Beau, aren't we?" she whispered, rolling her cheek against his silky coat. "And now we're going to show them some more."

10

Ox Ridge's annual show was just about a month away and, as it happened, was scheduled to have as a featured event the New England Belgian Shepherd Club's specialty show—as large a gathering of the breed as would be held in some time, and an important one for any dog being shown in the conformation classes. On something in the spirit of a lark, Isabelle entered Beau, in novice conformation, but her main concentration was on obedience, on the demanding events of the open class.

As the days lengthened rapidly into September, she and Captain Roberts drilled him off and on every day, either on the lawn or down at the beach. After Labor Day, it was empty, left only to such few wanderers as chanced to have their days at their own disposal.

By the week of the show, Beau was executing every move perfectly, without hesitation, with a showman's dash and confidence. And Roberts was elated and was even promising, after a half-dozen refusals, to show up at Ox Ridge on Sunday to cheer his friends on. "All right, Mrs. B. I guess you got me. I'm not one for hanging around, but if you want me there, well, I'll come. Wouldn't want the pup to think I'd turn my back on him on his big day."

Peter had said he'd come, too, and even John and Alison succumbed to curiosity and promised to join them at the club and to bring the picnic. They and the Hutchinsons and Rog would come down to the house afterward for a barbecue and general celebration. By Thursday night, Isabelle was so keyed up that she could hardly stop talking. Peter hadn't seen her like that in years—worrying about the weather, wondering how many of the breed would show up for the specialty, fussing about whether he'd want to come with her or bring his own car and come later. It was confusing, but he found it rather engaging, too, and quite looked forward to seeing Beau and Isabelle in the ring. Since she hadn't told him, though, about entering Beau in conformation, he elected to settle for coming at a later hour.

But why, on Sunday morning, did she have to get up at five-thirty to feed Beau and give him a final grooming and get her things together? He could hear her, rattling around downstairs. He managed to drift back to sleep until, at seven-thirty, she came up to lay out her clothes and shower. As she slipped into a pair of tan pants, a madras blouse, and a navy blazer and sneakers, he came to, groggily and grumpily. It didn't help in the least that she looked terrific and obviously felt just fine.

"Sorry to be up and out so early, dear, and I'm sorry to wake you up, but I'm going to have to be out of here soon, and I'm going to need your help before I go," she said. So cheerfully.

He lurched into a sitting position, propped on his elbows, and blinked at her. "Okay. Okay. But can I have some coffee before I'm called on for anything else?"

"Sure. I'll go fix it right now. You duck your head under the tap and be down. I just want to run through the course once more with Beau before we go, that's all. One more time."

Great. Just his area of expertise. "Well, all right, but I'm not any good at the fine points of this, you know, so I'm worse than useless as a critic if he's doing something off the mark.

And can you get me a muffin, too?" he hollered as she started down the stairs.

He thrust his arms into his bathrobe, and padded downstairs in her wake, slumping into his chair and sipping gloomily at the cup of coffee she poured for him. Isabelle split a muffin, and popped it into the toaster for him, just as Beau whimpered at the door from the garage. She ran to let him in and, as she did so, bent to give him a generous patting and even a swift kiss on the top of his head. "What a good dog you are, Beau. We're going to have such a big day today, aren't we?"

"Wish you'd be that nice to me," Peter muttered.

"Oh for heaven's sake," she laughed. "If I had you that well trained, I probably would be. No, seriously, he needs a little extra today. He has been a good dog, and I'm proud of him—and even proud of me, for what we've done together."

His voice was dry. "Isabelle, I wasn't saying you shouldn't be. I was remarking that I could use some attention around here myself. For months, now, he's certainly had a fair share, but he's never much taken to me, and I'm feeling a little left out, that's all."

Isabelle said nothing until she'd buttered the muffin and slapped it down in front of him. She was inches from him, staring at him with a hardness in her eyes and a set to her jaw that Peter had never seen there. He was suddenly conscious of Beau, slightly behind her and to one side, in an attitude of protectiveness, almost menace. When Isabelle spoke, her voice was icy.

"Peter, I want you to listen to me. For Beau and me, this is a very, very important day, and we are not going to allow you to derail it by being belittling or demanding or just plain, ordinary, goddamned selfish. If anyone in this house has been lacking a fair share of attention all these years, it isn't you. It's me. I've been a good wife, and a good mother, and a good housekeeper, and all the rest of it. I've never bitched about the time you've spent away on business, or away for something else, or off on a tennis court proving whatever it is you think you're proving out there. But now that I've found something that interests me, and occupies me, and lets me meet a few new people, and makes me proud of my own achievements, then I think it is very fucking tacky for you to complain."

In thirty years, he'd seen many different sides of Isabelle, but this was a new one. Peter sat perfectly still, trying to take it in. She went on.

"Now, your house remains well kept. And your wife remains well behaved. And if you've had to get a few of your own meals, it has been very, very few. But I've got something that's mine, not yours and not ours, and that is exactly what you are carrying on about. So stop it. And if you want to know, Beau's a damned sight nicer than most people I know.

He's loyal and affectionate. So leave me alone...." Her control was slipping now, the tears beginning to slide down her cheeks, and she turned her back on him and walked to the sink, Beau whimpering in sympathy with his nose against her hand.

Peter cleared his throat, trying for the words that would calm the outburst rather than continue it. She was just nervous, he knew, about the show. Just all tied up in knots with it. That was all. Finally, quietly, in a voice expressing reason and husbandly kindness, he said, "Look, what I meant, in so many words, was something like, 'How about a hug for me, too?' That's all. I know you're nervous about the show, but I want you to know I'm really proud of you. Now give me that hug, and we'll run through the course one more time. I'm sorry."

He pushed his chair back, and moved to put his arms around her, to banish whatever had caused that brief flash of rage. But as he moved toward her, Beau, seemingly in play, grabbed the hem of Peter's bathrobe in his teeth and swung hard to one side, throwing him off balance. Obviously, the dog was as strung out as Isabelle. Stage fright, he guessed. It was catching, but it would pass by tonight. At least he hoped so. Running the course would do them all good.

Even with his unpracticed eye, Peter could tell that this final run-through was perfection itself, each retrieve straight and true, each return perfectly square, each exercise of the "stay" series performed without a suggestion of creeping or change of position. Isabelle didn't need to repeat a single command.

"Oh, Beau," said Isabelle when they finished, "you are perfect, absolutely." She ruffled his ears and his thick mane. "Isn't he handsome, Peter? They're good-looking dogs anyway, but he really is getting beautiful." She wasn't going to tell him about the conformation entry, but she could hardly resist a hint.

By then, it was nearly nine, and there was no more time for anything but tossing her things in the car, letting Beau get settled in back, and setting off. "Be careful," Peter said, waving, and then, as they vanished up the road, turning and walking heavily toward the house. He wasn't looking forward to the prospect of fetching his own breakfast, making the bed, and straightening the bathroom and kitchen. "All for a goddamn dog," he said to himself. Oh, well, he could get it done before it was time to meet Isabelle and the kids, and at least Alison had said she'd bring a picnic. But, in his own mind, he'd decided that the Buckinghams had had enough of the dog game, and that it was time to get out. Nothing was worth the kind of outburst this had driven Isabelle to. It was even making Beau snappish. Rog would be at the show today, and at supper tonight, and he'd talk with him, and try to get him to talk with Izzy.

Isabelle was speeding up Noroton Avenue, after an anxious check on her watch. "We've really got to hurry, Beau." she said. "Your novice class is at ten, and I'd like to get you checked in and groomed before you start. This part's easy. This is just for looks, not for brains, and you are such a handsome fellow." She reached over to touch him, and he seemed, tongue lolling, to be almost smiling back at her.

Right on Middlesex, toward the club, past signs pointing to DOG SHOW. "Let's watch where we're stepping when we get there. Some dogs just don't have your manners. Okay?" And then they were there—a confusion of tented areas packed with crates and grooming tables and a crush of dogs, owners, handlers, and spectators. There was an incredible assembly of mastiffs, also a specialty for today—it looked as if someone had called an audition for a horror movie, until Isabelle got close enough to realize that most of them were so gentle that they hardly seemed to be able to stay awake.

There were booths selling every manner of dog food, dog accessory, dog sculpture, dog stationery, dog crates, kennel equipment, dog jewelry, pedigree tracing services, every product or service imaginable or unimaginable. Barking, whining, howling, yowling, and human curses filled the air indifferently, and battered metal folding chairs surrounded roped-in rings that would contain the conformation events.

Isabelle parked the car at the shady end of the field, threw her bag over her shoulder and a blanket over one arm, and picked up the basket into which she'd tossed Beau's things and her own. Wandering toward the main tented area, Beau heeling free at her side, she nodded to people she'd seen at the other shows or around town, and finally found the registration desk, where she checked Beau in for his classes, picked up her sleeve numbers and a program, and learned that things were already running about fifteen minutes late. The kindly but harassed woman in charge of registration advised her to go over by the proper ring, finish grooming her dog, and just wait.

She found the ring not by the directions so vaguely given to her, but simply by casting about until she saw what seemed to be an astonishing number of nearly identical black dogs, each apparently groomed to perfection, each with pointed and alert ears, each with a fluffy mane about the neck, each with a sweep of feathered tail. As she got closer, the illusion that the dogs were identical died quickly, for the bitches were easily distinguishable as smaller, lighter, and less heavily maned, and faults not apparent at a distance became clear on closer inspection—feet too splayed, necks too heavy, muzzles too snipey.

Among the owners, she found a couple from Rye who were pleased to let her use their grooming table, after they'd put the finishing touches to their bitch, and who made more than pleasant remarks about every aspect of Beau's appearance and manner. They talked as she worked, pulling out loose hair with a nubby rubber pad, then going over Beau with a wire brush. He lifted each foot for grooming, and permitted her to do his tail. In the end, though, coming down from the table, he took the first chance he got to roll ecstatically on his back, so that it had to be done over again.

She and the couple from Rye, Donald and Eileen Buchanan, laughed at this, and at the foolish, doggy grin that Beau seemed to flash at them when he did it. They asked if she were going to breed him. It was evident that they thought he might someday make a suitable sire for a litter by their two-year-old bitch, Tralee, who had her C.D. and only one major to go for her championship. Isabelle explained that this was her first attempt at conformation.

"Not that I'm all that serious about it," she explained, "but with the specialty being held so close to home, I certainly couldn't pass up a chance to see how he'd stand up and what the other dogs were like." She stopped to consider. "I might breed him, but he's too young, and will be for a while. I did promise the Hutchinsons a chance at one of his pups if I ever did. They bred him, and now they're sorry they sold him to me. Do you know them?"

As it turned out, they not only knew the Hutchinsons but now spotted them coming across the ring, Brummel on lead, and waved them over. It hadn't occurred to Isabelle until now, but she realized that they too were after the elusive final major that would put Brummel over the top of his championship. Evvy seemed taken aback to see Beau, all groomed and ready for the ring. "What am I going to do with you," she said in dismay to Isabelle. "It's bad enough that you're all over obedience, but now you're over here, ready to see what you can do in this. Wouldn't you like to sell him back?"

Isabelle was embarrassed and apologetic. "With all these dogs here, I'm sure we won't go far enough to get in your way, Evvy. Don't worry about it. This is the first time we've ever even tried this. Now come on. Help me with this armband and watch my things. It looks like they're going to call the novice class."

"What are you doing in novice?" said Evvy. "You belong in puppy class. And where's Peter? And what are you using for baits?" Evvy took the armband, held it to Isabelle's sleeve, and struggled with the ties. Some of the dogs were already in the ring.

"Peter's coming later, with my son and his girl," she said, as she started for the ring. "I didn't want him to know about this until it was over. What are baits?" The judge was motioning the rest of the class into the ring and she had no time for Evvy's answer. She shrugged, grabbed Beau's new show lead, and slipped it quickly around his neck. Suddenly the contestants were in the ring, trotting their dogs clockwise and then counterclockwise. "Come on, Beau," she whispered. "Let's just do the best we can." Then they all stood and, one at a time, trotted their animals back and forth, up and down, so that any fault in their movement would show. Isabelle had the presence of mind to notice that the dog that went before her had a kind of crablike sideways motion, and it gave her some confidence. Beau, watching her eagerly for any sign of how he should behave, seemed to catch her rush of optimism and fairly pranced out, straight and true, his tail wagging slowly from side to side, his coat glinting in the sunlight, his ears alert for any whisper of direction or encouragement. Two ringsiders applauded when he finished, and Isabelle, as the next dog started off, gave him a quick pat and a "Good boy."

Next, the judge examined each of the dogs for soundness of teeth, feet, the set of bone under the luxurious coat. One was waved out for snapping when his owner touched his mouth to show the judge his teeth, and several seemed so bored by the routine as to be utterly listless. Beau, however, turned on the charm, opening his mouth when asked, lifting his paws for examination, not in the least put off by this new procedure. Several of the other owners were using the baits to which Evvy had referred—hard-cooked bits of liver waved to attract the interest of the dog and elicit an alert look—but Isabelle had none and Beau didn't need them.

Then it was time for another tour or two around the ring, under the deep scrutiny of the judge, who made an occasional comment to the steward who was helping her. As Isabelle began to relax, she could notice a little more of what was happening, and she realized that this judge seemed to be someone of importance. A stout woman in a flowered print dress and an uncompromising straw hat, she was evidently a visiting Belgian; some knowledgeable bystanders who were showing in later classes were saying, in awed tones, that she was considered *the* authority on the breed.

Now, gesturing at them one by one, the judge was directing some dogs to leave the ring, some to stay. Beau and Isabelle were still in, but uncertain what was happening, and wilting in the heat and the stern glare of that imposing judge. Isabelle wondered if staying was an altogether good thing. What had seemed like a lark as she filled out applications at the kitchen table now seemed merely uncomfortable and awkward. She focused for a moment on Evvy, who was standing at ringside with Tom slightly behind her, and she could see that she was frowning in either distress or concentration.

Novice, indeed, Isabelle thought wildly, a trickle of sweat tracing its way down her back. *I'm the novice here.* The other remaining exhibitors looked cool and professional to her, and that made her feel worse.

Now the judge stalked back toward them, and had each repeat the paces and the inspection. Her face, heavy and ruddy in the heat, did not in any way change expression as she worked. She clearly took this as seriously as a doctor took surgery—even this unlikely occupation in this unlikely setting. Finally, with a sigh, she picked up a white ribbon, handed it to the owner of one of the other dogs, and shook his hand. Then the yellow, then the red. There remained the blue ribbon and a small trophy and, confused, Isabelle found herself fighting tears, thinking that her beautiful Beau could be eliminated now, in front of all these people. She let her hand stray to the smooth place between his ears, and he lifted his muzzle to lick her hand. Maybe it was against the rules. She didn't know and she couldn't have cared less, but the least she could do was give him a smile. But as she lifted her head, the judge was coming toward her, a broad smile on her face, the blue ribbon and the small metal trophy in her hand.

The woman was saying, "Very young animal, madame, so it is difficult to decide for him, but his condition is magnificent, and he is a most spirited youngster...though he should perhaps have been in puppy class. The breed competition is at half after twelve. Please see the steward about it. A fine animal indeed."

Stunned, Isabelle shook her head and accepted the ribbon and trophy, and then she simply sat down in the middle of the ring and hugged Beau, to the applause of the spectators. Scrambling to her feet, she spotted Evvy at the side of the ring, applauding and smiling broadly. To one side was Amos Roberts, grinning with satisfaction, a big dog biscuit held high in one hand. She made her way to him, and reached over the ropes to give him a victory hug, which turned out to be a little like falling face down on a broom. Beau lay down and demolished his dog biscuit while she tried to persuade Roberts to come and meet the Buchanans and the Hutchinsons, or at least to join her for the picnic later, but he would not, and seemed intent only on finding out where and when the next event would be. "Got to have your rooting section alongside, Mrs. B. I'll be there," he said, and retreated into the swirling crowd. She made her way out of the ring, and over to Evvy.

Out of breath with the heat and the excitement, she asked urgently if she had to show up at the twelve-thirty class. "Peter and John and Alison will be here by then, and we still have the open competition to go, and they're going to think I'm nuts," she said hopelessly.

Evvy was stern. "Well, of course you have to show up. That's what you entered for, isn't it? No one's going to think you're nuts. Now go find yourself some water for Beau, and something cold for you, and some shade. I've got a few minutes before Brum's class. I'll go with you."

Evvy's proprietary air had reasserted itself, and she steered them—Tom trailing with Brummel and a collection of possessions—to the south end of the field, under the trees that shaded the club driveway. "It's nearly eleven now, so it won't be that long before you have to get him ready. I'm going back to get Brummel set up, but if we see Peter, we'll tell him where you are and send him over. Keep an eye on the time."

Isabelle stretched out on the blanket under the tree, Beau beside her with his water, and she with her cup of lemonade. The blue ribbon fluttered from the handle of her basket, and the small trophy glittered among the more mundane brushes and oddments.

She reached out and touched his paw. "Well, Beau. What do you think of yourself? I've always known you were the most beautiful dog there was, but now you have the blue ribbon to prove it. So I owe you one steak for that, and one more for anything else you happen to pick up today. You make me so proud, but even if you were just a muttnik from the pound, you'd be better company than anyone I know."

She gazed squarely into his understanding brown eyes. Beau moved closer to her, put his great head on her arm, and sighed.

"Isabelle!" The voice came from far off. "Isabelle!" It was Peter, with Johnny and Alison trailing behind with the picnic gear. With a hug for John, and a smile for Peter and Alison, Isabelle showed them the morning's booty, explaining her secret entry in conformation and Beau's win. John thumped her on the shoulder, calling her Supermom, and spent a few minutes making friends with Beau, who didn't seem much interested. Peter, though full of the proper words of praise and congratulations, looked glum. This success would intensify Isabelle's interest in showing Beau.

The time was fast approaching noon, which meant another go at Beau's coat and a foray for spectator chairs, John and Alison leading the way. Peter picked up Isabelle's things, and walked with her back to the ring area where, wonder of wonders, the stout Belgian judge had managed to bring the other classes in something like on time. At 12:35, the winning males from puppy, novice, American-bred, bred-by-exhibitor, and open classes assembled in the ring under her expert eye. Evvy and Brummel were there from the open group, and Isabelle, who'd barely wanted to see Beau emerge the winning dog, suddenly realized that it couldn't mean as much to her as it would mean to the Hutchinsons. There was barely time to think about it, for again each dog was gaited and examined, several times. It seemed to take forever, but finally the judge handed Evvy the coveted purple ribbon. "For himself, Mrs. Hutchinson, because he is a fine dog, in every way, but also because he has proved himself in this pup of Mrs. Buckingham's."

That was it, Brummel's championship, and the applause from the Hutchinsons' friends swept the ring. Winner's bitch and best of opposite sex went to the Buchanans' Tralee, finishing her championship as well, and Brummel went on to represent the breed, as best of breed, in the working-dog class competition.

At this point, the Buckinghams, the Hutchinsons, and the Buchanans found a kind of instant victors' camaraderie, helped along by a cooler full of beer that the Buchanans had brought along. They too, were invited to join the barbecue at the Buckinghams, and said they'd be delighted to come.

Roger, wandering on his rounds of checking eligibilities, clapped them all soundly round the shoulders, mooched a beer, patted the dogs, and congratulated himself once again on being responsible for getting Isabelle there in the first place. But by then it was time for her to get some help from Alison in changing the number on her sleeve, and to join Beau's obedience class in number four position. As they walked to the north end of the area, she realized that the heat and the humidity were getting to everyone. The day had grown blistering and there was evidence that tempers were fraying.

As their competition got under way, the second entry—the Miss O'Toole that she'd met at Rog's hospital some months before— had to be asked to leave the ring. Flushed and exasperated, the woman had been yelling at her little cairn. "How embarrassing," Alison murmured.

"Some people just aren't prepared, or they take it too seriously, I guess," said Isabelle.

"Some dogs," said John with mischief in his eyes, "don't know when they should bite the hand that feeds them."

In the course of the competition, two more dogs, an eager springer and a labrador, broke on the down-stay, and had to be led away. By the end of the exercise, only Beau and a handsome Irish setter who'd worked perfectly with his teenaged owner had escaped without obvious faults. Beau was first, with 198, and the setter second, with 190—marked down for breaking slightly at the examination. With that, Beau gathered a second ribbon, a second trophy, the first win toward his C.D.X.—and the firm prospect of two fine steaks. Finished for the day, the Buckingham party straggled toward their cars and home. Rog, the Hutchinsons, and the Buchanans would join them later.

Isabelle's car was in a different direction altogether from the others, since she'd arrived so early, but she took her things and, with Beau trotting off leash alongside her, set out.

Suddenly, Miss O'Toole stood threateningly in front of her, shouting at her. "I know who you are, Mrs. Buckingham. I know there is something unnatural in the way you work with that dog. You're cheating, that's what you are, and I've filed a complaint with the committee. I'm going to catch you at this, you mark my words."

It was so preposterous that Isabelle could only laugh, but the sound died in her throat. The woman had completely forgotten her dog, which looked exhausted, confused, perhaps on the verge of heat stroke. And there was something chilling about the look in this woman's eyes—something crazy, really, in the hoarse voice, the flying hair, the shirt pulled loose from the band of her skirt, the sweat stains spreading under her arms. Involuntarily, Isabelle took a step backward, and looked to see if she could spot someone she knew. No one was in sight. If only she'd been able to persuade Captain Roberts to come with her.

As calmly as she could, with as much logic as she could muster, she said, "Please, Miss O'Toole. It's been a long, hot day, and I know you're disappointed at what happened in the competition. But I've trained my dog myself, in conventional ways, and I didn't cheat. But I don't yell at him, or threaten, and if you'd try the same approach, I think you'd get better results. Really. I'm sorry about this, and I know you will be, too, when you're feeling a bit better." She was trying to keep her voice firm, but this woman had rattled her, no question about it. Miss O'Toole took another step toward her, and she half jumped backward, turning her ankle slightly, and half falling. Then, from somewhere nearby, she heard an unearthly noise.

In the nearly seven months that she'd owned Beau, he'd barked occasionally, and on that one day, the day she'd asked him to go for the rake handle, he'd snarled. But this was different. This was a growl that came from deep in his throat—loud, steady, deep, and unnerving. The hair on his spine, his whole mane seemed to stand out, and his lips curled back, revealing long curved white teeth and red gums. He was staring, positively glowering, at Miss O'Toole, crouched as though to spring. Otherwise, he made no move. The little cairn took what refuge there was behind his mistress, pulling her back with him, her face now ash white rather than flushed. "Vicious, too!" she said as she moved away.

Isabelle took a moment to collect herself, leaning against a nearby parked car. "Think of that poor dog," she said to Beau, "having to live with a person like that." She shuddered. "I hope we don't run into them again, don't you?"

It was a very pleasant evening, the day's bad moments forgotten, the little row of trophies and ribbons on display, Peter presiding over the steaks and Rog over a makeshift bar, the four dogs frisking on the lawn as the light faded, and devouring any tidbit tossed to them good-humoredly, without interfering with one another. As the women cleared the plates away and made the coffee, however, Peter asked Roger to come back into the study for a private chat. And Beau left the other three dogs and trotted alone through the darkness.

He left the property, head low to the ground, using the thick grass alongside the Zieglers' fences for cover. There was little moon, and, given the blackness, he was all but invisible. The distance was less than a mile, and he covered it quickly, slipped past the Robertses' wall without being seen, and found Ellen O'Toole's little cairn asleep on the porch of her cottage.

As it started to rise, Beau seized it by the neck, stifling its bark. With a flick of his head he tossed it high and to one side. The little dog hit the edge of the porch with a thud and a dull crack, and rolled on its side like a broken toy. It had no chance to feel anything, no fear and no pain. Beau sniffed, and licked a trickle of blood from the side of the animal's mouth. Then he retraced his steps home and was there, snapping bits of steak from Isabelle's fingers, before anyone had remarked on his absence.

In the study, Peter was getting nowhere with Rog. "Oh, for God's sake, Peter, let her have her fun," he was saying.

"I don't like it, though, Rog. Dammit, I don't. He doesn't like me, and this is taking up so much of Izzy's time and interest."

"What you don't like, you damned fool, is not the way the dog acts toward you, but the way that Isabelle got out and about this morning without making you a four-course breakfast and doing the housework, that's all. That's a great dog. Of course she's devoted to him. And she's a great girl. My suggestion to you, if you can't share this part of her life, is to let her have her fun and to stop being selfish about it. God knows, you've had the tennis for years without her ever grousing this way. Not to mention the other."

"Rog, that's not fair," Peter shot back.

"Look, I know that. But try to see it this way: pretty soon he'll have won anything worth winning, and she'll have to retire him. So cheer up, and let's go back to the party."

Ellen O'Toole rose stiffly from the armchair in which she'd been reading and went to summon her little dog for the night. It was a minute before she understood the meaning of the odd, stuffed-doll angle of its head, and its total lack of response. And another moment of total shock before she stifled a sobbing scream and gathered the stiffening gray brown body tenderly in her arms.

11

Peter was not going to give up. The next morning, over breakfast, he broached to Isabelle the subject of Beau's retirement. "I spoke to Rog about him last night, and he seemed to think you didn't have much left to win, once you've got the C.D.X. and probably the championship out of the way. They should certainly be easy enough. Now that Brummel's retiring, Beau will probably clean up fairly quickly, and then I'll be seeing a little more of you both—and maybe even getting into it myself with one of Beau's pups." This seemed like the safest tack to take, just the right combination of urging and taking for granted.

"I might breed him, I suppose," she said indifferently. "The Buchanans would certainly like to mate him with Tralee when the time comes, and I know Evvy'd love to have a pup from that breeding."

Better than he thought. Now he could afford to be expansive. "Well, I guess it's settled then. A couple of more months, and then, except for special things—like if you want to take him to Westminster—he'll be finished with competition."

Now the edge was back in her voice. "I didn't say that, Peter. We enjoy the competition, and we're going to keep on competing. And I'm not going to have another pup. I'm happy with just Beau, and I think any other pup would be bound to be a disappointment."

"Anything you like, dear," said Peter. "I didn't mean to offend you. But I do wish we had more time together, that you could travel with me a little, and things. Maybe you could leave Beau with Evvy or the Buchanans for a little bit, and do that. I'm supposed to go over to France in March, to set up that new plant we're building. I'd love to have you with me—three, four weeks in France. Wouldn't that be nice?"

There was derision in her answer, when finally she answered at all. "Peter," she said, "I don't know what you want me to do. I don't want to have another fight, but you have to know that there's no point in my going to France. You know you'll kill yourself with work for the entire time, and that you'll sit around chewing your fingernails and waiting for spare parts to come in from the States. You know you'll be up until all hours supervising, the installation. That's how it'll be. That's how it always was and how it always will be." She paused and drew a long breath. "If you'd take a real vacation, if we could take Beau and go up to the Vineyard for a couple of weeks, that would be one thing. But there's no point in this."

"So it's Beau. Christ! I wish we could talk about something besides Beau. I wish..."

Isabelle's last shred of control had snapped, and she slammed her coffee cup into the sink, shattering it. "No. No. NO! You don't want me with *you*. You want me without *Beau*. Well, love me, love my dog, God damn it. What you want is for everything to be as convenient for you as it ever was. That's all you want. Well, I'm not going to leave him with anyone, for any length of time, and you can go to France or go to hell!"

There was a silence.

"Isabelle, Isabelle. Listen to me," he said at last. "Maybe there's some compromise solution to the thing. We've never had a problem we couldn't solve. But, please, cut out this competitive thing. For your sake and mine and his. How much can he enjoy this? Really?"

She was not to be mollified. "What you're caring about, as ever, is Peter. Whether you have someone you can snap on Thursday night and snap off Monday morning. You don't want me to travel with you. You didn't like it when I did. It cramped your style—which certainly, from the signs I read, hasn't been cramped any too much lately. As to competing—I may continue, and I may not. But I'll decide. He's my dog, and I'm my own person, for the first time in years. And he's not the problem. We're the problem, and it's too late to solve that. Now, go catch your train or you're going to miss it. I'm not going to discuss this again." She sagged, suddenly, with the burden of what she'd said, but she was in control now—no tears, and no regrets. Beau had moved to her side again, and was sitting next to her, gazing alertly at Peter.

The minute Peter rose from his chair and took a step forward, wanting somehow to apologize, to touch her hair and say he was sorry, Beau interposed himself between them, and a low growl rumbled in his throat. Another step forward, and his lip curled back, revealing his teeth. For the first time, Peter was afraid of him, so afraid that he had to struggle to conceal it. This was no time to tangle with Beau or Isabelle. And Isabelle was right—he'd miss his train if he didn't leave. Even now, he could hear a garbage truck coming up the Point, and in a minute, it would block the driveway.

So he grabbed his jacket, picked up his bags, and paused for just the briefest of moments in the doorway. "I'm sorry," he said. "Maybe you're right, Isabelle. Have a good week, and I'll see you Thursday." And then he was gone.

When the car was out of sight, she poured herself another cup of coffee, ruffled Beau's ears, fixed his breakfast, and watched him wolf it down. When he was finished, he came over to her, and put his head in her lap, closing his eyes blissfully as she scratched behind his ears and crooned to him, "What a fine dog! What a fine dog you are." She bent down to touch her cheek to the top of his head, and held it there for a long minute. "You know something, Beau? People mean something bad when they say someone's a son of a bitch, but I've never met anyone nicer than you." She laughed at that. "I mean, you're loyal, and you're brave, and you're beautiful. And you don't go around barking at people all the time. But Peter—well, I guess that's why he doesn't like you. But let me tell you, there's nothing he can do. I'm not going on any of his stupid trips, and I'm not putting you in a kennel, and I'm not getting any other dogs. I love you, Beau, and we're going to stick together, no matter what." She gave him an extra pat, and checked her watch.

"Come on. I've got to get cleaned up and dressed and at this house before Captain Roberts gets here. Can't just sit around here all day playing with my dog and hating my husband." She went upstairs to take a shower.

Beau, left to himself, prowled from the kitchen to the dining room, paused restlessly in the living room, and then continued into the foyer and up the stairs. Finding the bathroom door shut, he scratched at it, whimpering, but met no response, since Isabelle could not hear him. He sniffed at the bed, briefly, and then wandered down the hall, pacing it off, and returned. At the top of the stairs, he lay down, listening, head on paws, his ears swiveling. Then he went down the stairs again, and into the study. Isabelle's chair stood where it had been the night before, the frame slightly to one side where Peter had moved it after the guests had departed. Next to it, at an angle that left the two facing one another, sat Peter's chair. Beau sniffed at it, touched it with one graceful paw, circled it twice. As he did so, he went rigid. His neck was extended, his head was down, his tail almost straight, the hair all along his spine standing up. Again the low growl rose from his throat, a sound so primitive and so threatening that it would surely have chilled anyone who had been there to hear it. But no one was.

Suddenly, as though the chair itself were his adversary, he attacked it, tipping it to the floor. Growling and snorting, he slashed at it with his teeth, cutting the leather, raking the stuffing with his claws. Anything that resisted him, he wrenched apart, bracing with his paws and yanking with his teeth, until the chair was completely gutted. He backed off, panting from the exertion, and surveyed his victim. The leather upholstery hung in shreds from the frame. The kapok stuffing hung in gray wads through the leather and the backup muslin, and some of it drifted slowly in the early morning sunshine and settled lightly on the floor.

He lay down alongside Isabelle's chair, his accustomed place, to wait for her. The moment he heard her step on the stairs, he was wholly alert. When she reached the landing, she called him. "Beau, where are you?" He whimpered. "In the study. Okay. I have to clean up in there anyway." She put down the laundry she'd been carrying and came to the door.

The dog's ears turned toward her at the gasp, but he did not look up. "Oh, Beau!" she said. "What did you do?" She sat down in her own chair for a moment, trying to take in what had happened, and leaned down to give him an absent pat. "Well, Beau, I'll grant you one thing. He *has* been a stinker lately, you're absolutely right about that, and he's just damned lucky you didn't go after something more than his chair."

She put her arms around him to show that she wasn't angry. "It's okay, Beau. Okay. But I'd better clean this up right now, and you can go outside while I do it. What a mess! He'd be absolutely furious if he found out, so we'll just make sure he doesn't."

She got up, let Beau out the kitchen door to the garage, and got down her vacuum cleaner, a whisk broom, and some brown paper grocery bags, and then she rummaged for a tack-puller, and took everything back to the study.

First, she gathered up as much of the loose wadding as she could. Then, one by one, she pulled the tacks and staples that held the leather in place underneath the chair and held the buckram against the springs. She pulled it all away as best she could, tearing it where she had to, stuffing the wadding that came from behind it into the bags as she went. She worked for an hour before she was ready to cut the jute webbing and the strings that held the springs in place, and to remove the last of the upholstery so that the frame stood bare. She sighed as she straightened up, remembering that the garbage had already been picked up. She carried the bags out, and vacuumed up what was left. Finally, puffing, she called Beau, gave him a dog biscuit, and sat down with a fresh cup of coffee.

"Oh, Beau," she said, "I'm about half tired out, and all I've done is clean up the mess. Well, Captain Roberts will be here in a while, so I'll finish cleaning up the house before he gets here, and fix our lunch. Then maybe he can help us carry the chair out to the car so I can get it up to the upholsterer this afternoon. But you know what I'm going to have to do? I'm going to have to finish the bargello pieces by the end of the week, or we're going to get found out. And what a job that's going to be!"

She rushed through the rest of the morning, cleaning up, and slicing some cold steak and tomatoes for lunch. Roberts had left himself out of the barbecue yesterday, and she'd make it up to him with something really nice. A little past noon, he walked his bike down the driveway. She had just finished putting some flowers in a low bowl for the kitchen table, and she rushed to the back door to welcome him. He was simply beaming, and took her hand in his two big ones, saying, "Mrs. B., you and the big fellow really did it yesterday. Made me proud. Haven't had such a good time in a coon's age, watching him do so well. Where is he? Brought him a present."

But Beau didn't need to be called. He barreled through the kitchen door and jumped up, whimpering in delight, and licking old Roberts's face, nearly knocking him down. Roberts braced himself in the doorway, and retrieved from his pocket an enormous rawhide bone, complete with tag and faintly grubby ribbon, which he quickly stripped off and handed to Isabelle. The bone he held out so Beau could grab it, and Beau took it, powerfully but gently, in his jaws. He managed to bark past it, tossing his head from side to side, and waving his tail in salute before he retreated to his private cave under the table and began to work on demolishing his gift.

"Oh, Captain Roberts, we both thank you for that. And for everything. We'll skip the lesson today, and just have lunch—a little celebration for the three of us. How would that be?"

"Anything you say, ma'am. Can't see he needs a lesson at all. He'll take those next two shows same as he did that one," he said.

When they'd finished their lunch, and had each had a second cup of coffee, Isabelle asked him to help her with the chair. "One of the guests dropped an ash on this last night, and it scared me half to death. I was so afraid it would start a fire that I just took the whole thing apart," she explained. "I'll be glad to see it out of here." Together, they carefully maneuvered the chair out of the study into the foyer, and from there to the front step, onto the lawn next to the driveway, and there let it rest for a moment. Isabelle backed the station wagon around, and they tipped and pushed the chair in, and finally slammed the door with a sigh of relief. It seemed like a plausible lie, and she hoped it would work as well on Lombardi, the upholsterer. He was usually a man who worked on things for which time had been reserved long in advance. Worth a try anyway.

When Roberts had departed, she picked up

her bag and Beau, and drove into town to Lombardi's shop. She pulled into the driveway, swung open the tailgate of the station wagon, and went purposefully to the door of the workshop. Once inside, she simply waited for Lombardi to notice her.

"Mrs. Buckingham," he said finally. "What brings you here?"

She gestured helplessly toward the car, hoping it would work. "Oh, Mr. Lombardi, it's my husband's chair. We had guests last night, and one of them burned a hole in it—really a bad one. After I'd put out the smoldering, I was so scared of it that I just stripped it, right down to the frame. It's out in the car. I thought that maybe if I brought it in, you'd be able to work on it. I've almost finished the new upholstery for it. I've been working on it ever since you drew the patterns for me, but I should be done by Friday."

His gesture was extravagant, quintessentially Italian. He was, at least to some extent, resigned to the capricious ways of his customers. "Let me see," he said. "You have brought it all the way here, and I will look."

And, to her relief and gratitude, he had one of his strapping apprentices carry the bare frame into the shop, on her promise that they could start the refinishing now, and have the upholstery pieces by the end of the week.

A couple of errands and about an hour later they were home again, with time only for a quick reprise of the course before Isabelle felt ready to sit down and see if she really would be able to finish the pieces by Friday. She was working on the back now, and had only a few inches to go, but then she'd need to do a couple of rows of stitching around each piece before they'd be ready for Lombardi. What she had ahead of her would ordinarily have taken her a couple of weeks, working a bit at a time, and she thought that she should get them out of the house by Thursday, three days away.

"Okay, Beau," she said. "You can go outside, or sit right here, where Peter's chair was. I'm going to pull the frame around and see how far I can work today."

It was three when she began, and five-thirty before she finished the last of the bargello and stopped for a while, rubbing a sore back and blowing on her fingers. She was remembering that she should have learned, long ago, to use a thimble.

"Beau," she said, "I'm as stiff as a board. Let's walk down to the beach before supper. That'll get the kinks out, and then we can have a drink and some supper and work on this some more." He rose eagerly, looking up at her with an almost quizzical expression on his face.

"Don't worry about it," she said. "It's all right, and I'm not angry at you. You've never done a bad thing in your life. We had to get the chair fixed anyway, and he'll never find out, so it won't hurt." She bent and brought her cheek down next to his head. "Of course I love you. Now let's go. It's going to be dark soon."

Down by the water it was deserted, as they made their way across the parking lot and out to the jetty. There, Isabelle stretched out on the rocks and relaxed, glad for Beau to have a run while she had a rest. She closed her eyes and thought how easy it would be to sleep, to feel the soreness seep out of her and to listen to the waves and drift with their sound. But there was so much left to do. She opened her eyes, and saw Beau off down the beach, playing with a clump of seaweed. She called him and got up, and together they started home.

Once there, she poured herself a drink, fixed Beau's supper, and put on some soup for herself. Then it was back to the study, back to the stitching. With only the edging to go, it seemed to her as though it should go faster, but when she broke for supper at eight, she felt that she'd hardly made any progress at all. Her fingers were red and sore, and her back ached. She rummaged through the kitchen drawers and cupboards, and emerged with a pack of cigarettes and some brandy.

"This will get us through, Beau," she said, putting her soup bowl in the dishwasher and heading back to the study. "I'll break every hour or so for some brandy and a cigarette, and that way I'll just keep on going till I'm done."

Even so, when she stopped, exhausted, at

eleven, she had less than half the edging done. She laid all the pieces out on the floor, all of them retrieved from the plastic bag into which she'd slipped them, one by one, as she'd finished the bargello. Through a cloud of smoke, and with another brandy in her hand, she surveyed the work so far. "Well, I'd guess I have another whole day of work, but they don't need blocking, thank God, and if they do I'm sure Lombardi can do it," she said to Beau. "And they're pretty. Peter should be grateful to you for spurring the project on, right? Now let's get them all back in the bag and take a walk and go to bed. I've had it."

She stepped outside with him, into a clear, cold starry night that cleared the cobwebs from her head. She was, she realized, a little tight from the brandy and the fatigue. After a few minutes she yawned widely. "You ready, Beau? I feel scruffy, and I'd like to take a quick shower before bed. Okay?"

He came and stood next to her, and they walked back into the house. She went around, locking the doors and checking the windows, before she went upstairs to turn down the bed, undress, and step into the shower. When she came out of the bathroom, toweling herself dry, Beau was sleeping not in his accustomed place on the floor beside the bed, but stretched out along Peter's side of it. She leaned over to stroke him.

"You just stay where you are," she whispered. "It won't hurt anything, and you look too comfortable to move. That's fine. It's even kind of an improvement." And a minute later, falling asleep, she reached out and put one arm around the big dog's neck. It made her feel perfectly safe, and she fell instantly asleep.

12

The next morning she went into town to pick up a thimble. She'd have to use it now. The middle finger on her right hand was pierced and swollen. Stopping only to run Beau through the course when Captain Roberts came by around eleven, to walk to the beach and back a couple of times, to eat or to have some coffee, she worked all day Tuesday, until after midnight, and all day Wednesday, until finally each piece lay stacked perfectly on the desk behind her, completely finished. When she'd talked to Peter on Tuesday night, she'd told him that the chair was gone and that she'd finished the pieces. It had driven her on to finish, made her do it to keep her story intact. They were beautiful, no question about it, but she was too tired to care. She stretched out on the floor, flat on her back, and enjoyed being at ease for the first time since Monday morning. Beau, who had not left her side at all, stood up and walked stiff-legged to her. He whimpered and licked her face softly, poking her shoulder experimentally with one graceful paw.

"Oh, Beau, no need to look so sympathetic. It had to be done, and it is. Let's go for a walk as soon as I've finished just lying here. I'm really okay." She touched his mane. "You are a faithful fellow, you know. I can't think of a single person in the world who would have sat here with me these last two days. What do you say to a walk, and then we'll drive up to Howard Johnson's and get some ice cream? You like it as much as I do, even if it isn't on your regular diet. Tomorrow we can exercise it off, right? And we have a show on Saturday."

It felt good to be in the car, to feel the night air. Beau waited for her while she bought the ice cream, an expectant look on his face, knowing he was in for a rare treat. Back home, she put two scoops in his bowl, and one in hers. "Funny sort of party, old Beau, for two early-to-bedders like us," she said when they'd eaten it all. He thumped his tail, either in agreement or in quest of another scoop. She put the bowls in the sink and said, "No, no more tonight. Maybe tomorrow. Let's have a little stroll, and then we'll set the alarm so we can get up to Lombardi's first thing tomorrow."

Once again, that night she let Beau sleep on the bed. This time, as she fell asleep, it was to the soothing sensation of his licking the swollen fingers of her right hand, his soft breath warm against her arm.

She woke early the next morning, feeling marvelous now that the work was over. She showered quickly, dressed, and put the upholstery in the car, thinking that she'd get there first thing, right after eight, but that she'd indulge herself first by picking up the papers and having breakfast at the little bakery around the corner from Lombardi's—the one with the best coffee in town. So it was just before seven-thirty when she backed out of the garage and slammed the overhead door down. Back in the car, she gave Beau a hug, and said, "Look, we're done. We did it!" Going up the Point, they passed the garbage truck. "Now," she said, "there's the nice man who's going to dispose of the evidence."

But the garbage man, tugging at the door, called to the driver. "Damn thing's stuck, and that was the missus we passed up the road there. Have to leave it till Monday. Gimme something, so I can write her a note." He scrawled his apology, and wedged the note in the side of the door. Inside, where he could not see, one of the overhead supports had worked loose, and the roller had left its track on one side, wedging the door shut tight.

In the bakery, Isabelle selected coffee and

blueberry muffins, and settled down with the morning paper. Beau, under the table on the floor, was there in violation of health regulations, but no one seemed to care. "Cleaner than most people," she was apt to say. Drawing out the time it took her to drink two cups of coffee, she stayed until just after eight, paid her bill, and departed.

"Dear Mrs. Buckingham," he said, "you are very prompt, but I fear you've done a lot of work that we won't be ready for for a little while. We have first to do the finishing, then the new springs and upholstery before we can fit the new covers. But they are beautiful, and you will be proud of the work, I promise."

"Don't worry about it, Mr. Lombardi," she said. "I've worked so long on these that I just wanted to get them done. I'm just pleased to turn it over to you."

She was annoyed, but not really alarmed, to find the note on the garage door. Mallory, the handyman, said he'd be able to come by around four. In the meantime, she could clean up the house, and do something special for dinner. Maybe have the Hutchinsons and the dogs down, if Evvy could get a sitter on short notice. Something fancy, maybe Chinese. She could go up to Westport and shop for ingredients. If the Hutchinsons could come then she wouldn't have to be alone with Peter all evening, and it would be like a party. She sat down and started making the necessary telephone calls, waited for Evvy to confirm with Tom and the sitter, and then started off to do her shopping.

Before Mallory had arrived, she'd done all the preparations for her Szechwan shredded beef and stir-fried vegetables. Mallory took only an hour to repair the damaged door. After he left, she decided on a long, luxurious bath, a short nap, and her best hostess gown. That would do it.

By six-thirty she was dressed and downstairs, hurrying to get glasses and things for drinks together on a tray in the living room, and to set the dining room table. If they had drinks there, Peter wouldn't feel the absence of his chair so quickly. Well, it would be back soon enough. She fed Beau his dinner, switched the napkins and mats from damask to a bright blue and white weave. At five to seven, she heard Peter's train, and at seven exactly the Hutchinsons pulled into the driveway. As she was answering the door, Peter pulled around behind them. He seemed surprised but not upset to find that they had guests. She kissed him lightly on the cheek. "All a big stratagem to keep you from missing your chair, dear. I thought you'd be pleased."

He and Tom poured the drinks and waved the women off to the kitchen for a look at the preparations. But the cooking was all last minute, so the four of them could enjoy the cocktail hour, their dogs variously disposed around their feet. It was only when Evvy and Isabelle had finished the cooking and were bringing the dishes into the dining room that the conversation took a serious turn.

"Did you hear about what happened to Ellen O'Toole's cairn?" said Evvy. No one had. "Well," she went on, "I ran into Rog today, and he told me that Ellen had called him Sunday night. She'd gone to bring the dog in for the night and found it dead. He did an autopsy, and found that it had broken its neck—hardly a mark on it, either, poor thing."

"What had happened to it, then?" said Isabelle, suddenly on edge.

"That's the thing. Rog couldn't figure it out. If it had been hit in the road and injured like that, it couldn't have made it home. And it didn't seem to have been in a fight, either. She just found it dead, right on her own front porch."

"Who's Ellen O'Toole?" said Peter.

"Remember that woman who was disqualified on Sunday?" Isabelle said. "The one that was yelling at her little dog? She lives two doors north of the Robertses—not a very nice woman, I don't think, but what a dreadful thing to have happen." She would not mention the way the woman had come up to her after the show.

Evvy, more or less relishing her role as bearer of gruesome tidings, went on. "Rog says it's the sort of thing he's occasionally seen happen in a really awful dogfight, but never unless it was a bad one, and the dog was otherwise badly marked up."

"Lord, Evvy," Tom groaned, "not at dinner."

That, at least, was enough to get dinner served, and to submerge the conversation in compliments for a delightful meal. And afterward, over sherbet and coffee, the talk was all of the weekend upcoming, and Beau's fine prospects. A little after ten-thirty, the Hutchinsons left. Thursday was no night to party late.

When they were gone, Isabelle gathered up the dishes from the living room and dining room, and pulled a big apron over her gown. Peter lent a hand as she tucked things in the dishwasher and cleaned the serving dishes and the woks in the sink. "Is that it?" he said finally. "I guess I'll take the garbage out, then." He pulled the plastic liner from the can and twisted a wire closing around it.

In a moment, he was back, laughing, with a ragged piece of leather dangling damply from his hand. He held it up, and Isabelle felt her mouth go dry. "If this is your idea of craftsmanship, honey, I think you should have left it to Lombardi. You must have had an awful time getting the upholstery off that chair. It's ripped to shreds." He dropped a new liner in the can, and tossed the torn strip of leather into it.

Then he turned to her and smiled. "Look, I know this evening was your apology for what happened over the weekend, and I want to apologize too. Dinner was delightful, and you look absolutely grand. Once Tom got Evvy off autopsies, it was really nice. But come on, it's late, and we should be getting to bed."

Beau had been out while they did the cleaning up, so Isabelle let him in now, as Peter locked up. They went upstairs together and got ready for bed, but as Peter came out of the bathroom, he found Beau lying in what was normally his place. "Isabelle, speak to him, will you? He doesn't pay any attention to me, but I would like to get some sleep tonight, so ask him to get down."

For one rebellious moment she considered saying no. But at last she said, "Okay, Beau, that's all right when Peter isn't here, but you'll have to sleep in your regular place tonight, okay?" She slapped the side of the mattress with her hand, and Beau reluctantly got to his feet and dropped slowly to the floor, where he curled up with his back against her side of the bed.

Long after the lights were out, long after Isabelle's slow steady breathing told him that she was asleep, Peter lay in the dark. He had heard Beau move across the room. He was sure that the dog was staring at him, and he was uneasy that he could not see something that could see him. Only when fatigue overtook him entirely did he sleep, and then it was to dream of things so strange and threatening that he could not, did not want to, remember them when he awoke. The next morning, he felt as if he had barely slept at all.

13

Again that weekend and the next, Beau took top honors in both conformation and obedience. He had earned his C.D.X. and another major toward his championship, and was photographed for one of the dog magazines, surrounded by his trophies, Isabelle by his side. Peter, thinking that the show career was indeed winding down, was careful not to criticize and, with a heavy schedule of travel, had few opportunities to do so.

With a rainy spell in mid-October, Isabelle and Captain Roberts slacked off the training a bit. It was uncomfortable to work on the new series of scent discrimination exercises when the weather was so wet. For a month or so, they took it easy—Captain Roberts coming by for lunch or for tea and cinnamon toast when he could get out on his bicycle, or joining them for long walks on the beach when the weather was really fine.

And, of course, in Peter's absences, Beau

continued to sleep in his place.

Then, early in November, when the weather had turned from cool to downright cold, Mr. Lombardi called to say that he'd be bringing the chair that afternoon, if that was convenient for her. Isabelle was pleased, since Peter was due home, and the return of his much-missed chair would be the best surprise he could have. He'd grouched about it constantly for a month. During that time, she'd even used the left-over wool from the chair to make a matching footstool, which she'd upholstered herself and hidden away as an extra surprise. She'd have everything in place when he came home, just as always, instead of having their drinks in the living room.

Lombardi arrived around four and apologized for running late. It didn't matter. She'd have plenty of time afterward to run up to town and get something for dinner. "It couldn't look better," she said, pleased beyond measure as she peered into his truck. "Why, it doesn't look like the same chair!"

"Ah, Mrs. Buckingham, the compliments belong to you. Beautiful! I've been teasing my wife, trying to get her to do some, but I fear it would make the rugs look worn, and the curtains, and everything, and then I'd have to pay to have the whole thing done over. You watch, when I get this in the house, you'll feel the same way!"

But to Isabelle, it simply looked splendid, and when she'd pulled the footstool from its hiding place in the attic, it seemed just perfect. She fetched Lombardi's check, plus a bottle of Peter's finest red Bordeaux, and thanked him for a perfect job.

When he'd gone, she sat for a few minutes in her own chair, and admired what she and Lombardi had achieved. He'd been right, of course. She was going to have to do something about the rug and the curtains and her own chair. But it was no time to think about that. She'd better get up to town and do the marketing. First she brought in some wood and set a fire to light later, composing her shopping list as she worked. A tomato and shrimp salad with the anchovy dressing that Peter liked. A small steak, and french fries, which he'd devour even when he was—as he always seemed to be—watching his waistline. He always gained about five pounds in the winter anyway, no matter what. She straightened up and swept the hearth. It would be a perfect evening.

She washed her hands, dashed on some lipstick, and called Beau as she slipped into her coat. It was getting late and dark as she started for the car. She'd forgotten, as she was apt to do at this time of year, that the dark came on quickly after the end of daylight savings time. She flicked on the lights as she backed up the driveway.

She left Beau in the car while she shopped; for the fifteen minutes or so she was in the market, he'd be better off there than lying out in the cold, but he seemed oddly restless when she got back to the car.

When she began to pull out of the parking lot, she felt the wheel pull and heard the slapping of a tire gone flat. "Damn!" she said, as she got out of the car to look. Indeed, the right front tire was resting on the wheel rim. Beau walked with her the block to the closest gas station, looking for help. Finally the new tire was in place, but it had taken nearly forty-five minutes, and the old one was totally beyond repair. The attendant showed her why.

"Take a look, Mrs. Buckingham," he said. "The thing looks slashed. I'll put a new one on the rim, and you can pick it up tomorrow; but I think you ought to stop into the station house and report this." He probed the slit with his fingers. The station house was on her way. She stopped by and told the desk sergeant about it.

By the time she got back in the car, it was dark and beginning to rain again, the wind picking up from the northeast and sweeping the rain across the road. She flicked on the lights and the radio, and sang along with Carly Simon. "You're so vain.... You gave away the things you loved and one of them was me," she sang, wondering just how many women her age knew that one all the way through. As she zigged onto the Point, and zagged toward home, her headlights caught a rusty blue Volkswagen parked in the weeds along the inlet. "Some fishermen," she said to Beau, "seem to come out in any wind or weather. Brr!"

The rain was pelting down as she pulled into the garage, and the house was dark. "Let's get these things in and get you some dinner. Peter will be home before long, and I'm not even going to have time to change."

As Beau jumped down from the car, he sniffed the air warily.

"Come on," she urged, hurrying. "It's just dark. Nothing to be spooky about." She lifted the sack of groceries and her bag, fumbling for her keys before she remembered that she hadn't locked up. She'd meant to be gone only a few minutes; it had been more like an hour and a half. She shrugged, and reached for the doorknob, had her hand on it in fact, when the door was pulled slowly away from her from the inside.

For a moment, she couldn't breathe, and her legs threatened to give way.

The man was young, hardly more than a boy. She did have time to realize that as he opened the door and stood silhouetted in the near dark. But in his right hand was a pistol.

"Sorry, lady," he whispered. "I thought the tire would take longer than that. I was just leaving." Now she could see the shine of his leather jacket and could see the rucksack on his back, filled with God alone knew what possessions of hers. She sensed that Beau was no longer by her side, no longer anywhere near her.

"Now just put the groceries down, lady. Walk very slowly into the kitchen and put the groceries down. Don't turn on any lights, and keep your back to me, and move very slow. You got that? Good. Very slow now." He waved her in the door, training the gun on her as she walked shakily to the counter and eased the bag of groceries onto it. She could feel him staring insolently at her back.

"I'm not going to hurt you, lady. I'm pretty sure you can't identify me, so I'm just going to tie you up for a little bit so you can't tell the cops right away. Just long enough for me to get away, okay?" She knew his back was to the door, and with all her concentration she wished for Beau to hit him, and hit him hard, knew he'd have to put the gun down to tie her up and that that should be the time. There was a long, breathless pause as the man waited for her to answer.

But she never had to, for at that very instant, Beau was through the doorway, a shape detaching himself from the dark and launching himself with everything he had at the man's back. His weight sent him sprawling. His first move had been silent, but now there was a frenzy of growling, and above it, the man's scream of agony.

Still dazed and shaky, Isabelle was trying, in the confusion, to make her way to the light switch, when her foot struck the gun. She bent to pick it up, and was startled by the cold smoothness of it. Her father had taught her to shoot, years before, and it struck her that it was somehow going to be important, when the lights came on, to be holding it with a look of absolute authority. She adjusted it by feel, and, edging her way along the wall with her free hand, fumbled for the light switch. The sound of struggle had intensified. Mingled with the burglar's cries were throaty noises from Beau, and the sounds of fabric and leather tearing. Finally, and with enormous relief, she found the light switch and hit it.

What she saw made her stomach lurch. The young man was on his hands and knees, trying, against all odds, to drag himself to the door. His pants and jacket were torn to shreds, and covered with blood. One cheek had been slashed open completely, and from it the blood poured. The rucksack, still on his back, had skewed to one side, heavily laden, and kept thwarting his efforts to escape the enraged animal. Patches of blood smeared the floor and the cabinets and had spattered over Beau's coat. He stood over the burglar menacingly, growling, and looked up at Isabelle for guidance.

"It's okay, Beau. You're a good dog. Good dog."

"Mean as shit," said the young man, his voice hoarse with fear and pain.

"Not mean. Protective," said Isabelle. "Get up."

"I can't."

"Do it anyway. I've got your gun and my dog, and I'm telling you what to do." She didn't feel nearly as brave as she sounded. "I assume the gun is loaded. Is that right?"

He nodded slowly.

"Then do as I say. Now. Slowly." Beau growled again, and the man got painfully to his feet. He turned to face her, his eyes wide and dilated with terror, his lank dark hair falling forward over his eyes, the blood running freely down the slashed cheek.

She motioned him to a chair. "Get over there while I call the police. Beau will watch you do it." She stepped backward, toward the telephone, and groped for the receiver with her left hand. As he sat, with a sigh of pain and resignation, she lifted it, tucked it under her chin, and dialed the operator. "Darien police," she said. "It's an emergency."

The operator put her through right away, and the police promised to dispatch a patrol car and an ambulance. She'd barely had a chance to sag against the wall in relief before she heard the wail of a siren coming closer and then the crunch of the squad car's tires hitting the gravel in the driveway. The revolving lights danced on the walls, the doors of the car slammed, and two burly officers burst into the kitchen.

She'd thought she was fine, but actually seeing those big blue-clad men, well-armed, benevolent, clearly in charge, seemed to drain it all from her. She handed the gun to one of them weakly and said simply, "I'm so glad you're here."

While his partner leaned against the wall, laconically reading the burglar his rights before he began questioning him, the other officer guided her to a chair in the dining room, lit a cigarette for her when she proved too shaky to hold it, and began to ask her questions. Now that the officers were in charge, Beau sat down beside her and put his big head in her lap, whimpering and licking her hands. "Good dog, Beau. Good dog, and so brave. What would I have done without you, hmmm?" she said, the tears beginning to slide down her face.

"Now don't worry, Mrs. Buckingham. We're going to be here awhile. Look, I'm Officer Hurley, and my partner's Upton. Why don't I just find you a drink? He's going to be awhile, and I'll need to get your story, all right? Where's the whiskey? I'll fix what you want." She nodded gratefully, told him where to find it, and sat back, numb. When Hurley came back, she told him her story—going out to pick up something for dinner, the flat tire, getting it fixed, reporting it, coming home. She gestured to the gun, now lying on the table in a plastic bag, and then the tears started again. "I was so frightened, Mr. Hurley. I just couldn't believe what was happening, and there was one awful moment when I didn't know where Beau was...."

"He's a brave dog, ma'am. Okay to pat him, or is he dangerous?"

"No," she said, astonished. "He's a perfectly nice dog. He just knew something was wrong." Hurley reached out to stroke Beau but withdrew his hand, as if he were not quite sure of him, or shy of the blood, and then went back in the kitchen again.

A few minutes later, the ambulance arrived, and she could hear the attendant whistle and say, "Wow! I better clean him up a little." Then there was a thud, and some muttered curses, and the attendant said, "He's passed the hell out!" Then there was loud honking from the end of the drive. *It must be Peter,* she thought dully, *but let them handle it.*

Hurley ducked his head in the door. "Looks like your husband's come home, ma'am. I'll go up and ask him to park by the road until we're done here." A few minutes later, he brought Peter in, confusion and relief showing on his face when he saw that Isabelle was all right, shaken but all right.

Going into the kitchen to pour himself a drink before he joined her, he had to avert his eyes from the damage Beau had done, but he did pick up and relay the news that the burglar, one Jim Russo, had been responsible for a number of similar crimes in the area. It seemed that his technique was to park in a prosperous neighborhood, familiarize himself with the various cars, and then pull out behind a housewife who looked as if she was probably just picking something up in town and was unlikely to be locking the house. He'd follow her into a parking lot, slit a tire, and give himself time to go back and comb the house for valuables—getting out, most of the time, while the housewife was still waiting for repairs in a gas station in town.

Finally, the ambulance attendant had finished with Russo. He and Upton maneuvered the stretcher through the kitchen and dining room, out the living room, and through the front door. The officers thanked her, and promised to be back in touch soon. She nodded, and Peter, his arm around her shoulder, nodded, too.

"I'll walk you fellows out and get my car," he said. They plodded slowly up the drive. Isabelle watched them as the stretcher was lifted into the ambulance. She turned back to Beau. "You're a hero tonight, old fellow. Let's clean you up and get you some dinner," she said. So she was not there as Peter, standing by, took notice of the torn leather sleeve of the burglar's jacket which now, snipped free at the wrist by the ambulance attendant, hung loose at the side of the stretcher, empty of the pathetically thin and heavily bandaged arm that now lay across the burglar's chest. He stared at it hard, trying to imagine what it might be that it reminded him of, fighting the nausea that crept into his throat at the sight of the damage Beau had inflicted. He turned abruptly to Upton, who was about to climb into the ambulance.

"What did he take?" he asked.

"Not sure yet," he answered. "We'll do an inventory later. It's all in the rucksack. Hurley, here, will show you that and the gun, if you're interested. I'm sorry about this, sir, but your wife really handled herself well, and that's one hell of a dog. She'll feel better tomorrow. Just you wait and see."

Peter nodded, and let Hurley show him the bagged evidence. The sight of the gun, glinting a blue gray in the light from the roof of the patrol car, made him shudder. An evil object, only a short time before trained on his wife. He'd felt sorry for Russo before, but he damned well didn't now. No matter how badly hurt he was, and how scared, he'd pointed a gun at another human being, and he didn't qualify for pity.

He thanked them and said good night, and walked heavily to his car as both the other vehicles pulled slowly out of the driveway. Once they were gone, he backed up, and then swung forward, down the driveway and into the garage. He turned the engine off and slumped against the wheel. "Christ, am I tired," he said to himself. And then he opened the door and took his bags and went back in the house.

Isabelle was stretched out on the sofa in the

living room, her arm shading her eyes from the light, Beau by her side. Peter whispered her name, and her eyes fluttered open. "Not asleep, dear, just resting for a moment. It's been awful."

"Why don't I pour us each another drink and order a pizza, and you can tell me about it," he said.

She cracked a wan smile. "I have the feeling that I'm going to get tired of this story," she said, but she got up and went in the kitchen with him. The officers had cleaned up most of the mess, but she dabbed at some of the rest as he made the drinks.

"I'm better off busy," she said. "I think I'll fix the dinner. I never did get to put the groceries away." In a minute or two, she laughed. "I was going to say that it all started with your chair, but in all this confusion, you haven't even seen it. Come on!" she said, taking his hand.

Though they were both tired, it would have seemed inappropriate, somehow, not to sit for a while in the study after supper. Both of them made bad jokes about the need to redecorate around Peter's chair and footstool. Peter kicked off his shoes and stretched out luxuriously, his feet up on the new footstool, admiring Isabelle's handiwork and Lombardi's skill, and allowing that the chair—once broken in—would be as comfortable as it had been.

As he spoke, something nagged at him,

something like a forgotten line of a song, something familiar but just beyond his grasp. It made him restless. He got up, poured them each a brandy, let Beau out and then in again, and sat in his chair as Isabelle, relaxing a little, chattered.

"I know you wanted me to get rid of Beau, or stop showing him, or whatever. But I think if he'd never done anything else, he proved his worth tonight. If it hadn't been for him, I don't know what would have happened. He's a real hero," she said, swirling her brandy and having a sip. "The worst part of the whole thing," she went on, "was that moment that I didn't know where he was. He must have hung back in the darkness until the burglar turned his back to him." She trailed her hand over the arm of her chair and stroked Beau's back.

"Beau really savaged him," Peter said, after a moment. He got up and tossed another log on the fire, and waited until it caught.

"Peter? Do you mind if I have a cigarette before I go to bed?" she asked.

"I would ordinarily, but not tonight. Go ahead."

She got up, left the room, and came back with a pack and an ashtray, which she put beside her chair. She lit one, and smoked in silence for a few minutes, letting the smoke drift.

She sighed. "I guess in the morning I'm going to have to take inventory and then go up to the station house," she said.

"So I gather."

"Better finish this and my brandy and get to bed. How about you?"

"I think I'll just sit for a while and enjoy my chair," said Peter. "I'll lock up later." He paused.

"Isabelle, I know we've had our differences about Beau. No more. He's a fine dog and he may have saved your life tonight. I'm awfully glad you're safe." He rose to kiss her good night, lightly, and then she made a little chucking sound to Beau, who had been lying at her feet, and they were gone. He settled back into his chair to try to make the connection that had been eluding him all evening. Even with the help of another hour and another brandy, though, he could not. It would come to him, he supposed, but in the meantime, he'd better lock up and get to bed.

Well after midnight, awakening to the sound of wind and rain, Peter lay staring into the dark. He could remember himself holding up the scrap of torn leather from the chair and saying, "You must have had an awful time getting that upholstery off," and in his mind's eye, he could see the torn sleeve of Russo's jacket, swinging free from the side of the stretcher. The two pieces had been torn in just the same way. And if Beau had torn the one, he could have torn the other. And that meant that for some reason Beau had destroyed his chair, must have done it the morning after the Ox Ridge show, the weekend that he and Isabelle had fought so bitterly.

But why?

The dog never did anything that Isabelle didn't tell him to do, but he could not imagine her doing that, could not think it was possible. He tried to put it together, but try as he would, the pieces would not fit.

14

Friday morning, from his office in New York, Peter called Roger Stanley. He reached him at his hospital and, trying to keep the edge out of his voice, asked him casually how he'd been.

"Fine, Pete. Dandy. But that's not why you're calling. What's up?" said Rog. "Can I hope you have a new joke that's not for Isabelle's little pink ears or Beau's big black ones?" He laughed heartily at that, but this morning, he was his own best audience.

"Very funny, Rog," said Peter, "but I'm not in a joking mood. We had a burglar last night, some gun-waving kid, and Isabelle walked in on him. If it hadn't been for Beau, she might really have been hurt, but she's very shaken, and so am I."

"Christ. I'm sorry, Pete. I had no idea. You'd better tell me about it."

When Peter finished the recitation, Roger made a whooshing sound, part astonishment, part relief. "Well, what's the problem? It sounds like you have everything in hand. If you're worried about this kid suing you for what Beau did to him, he can't, so don't bother about it."

"Rog, it isn't that. It's something else and it's kind of strange. Right around the time of the Ox Ridge show, Isabelle and I had a couple of pretty bad spats about Beau. I went off on a trip, and while I was gone, she sent my chair out to be reupholstered. When I came home, I found some torn leather in the garage—really ripped up. I even teased her about it, but I didn't think much of it until last night. Beau had got at this kid pretty badly, and torn the leather jacket he was wearing. Just the way that piece of my chair had been torn. I think Beau did both. And I don't mind telling you that it makes my skin crawl. I mean, why would he do that?" He shifted in his chair, and leaned forward, as though by doing so he could force Rog to make some sense of this for him.

But Rog's voice was ripe with mock gravity. "Well, Peter my boy. If he did that to your chair—and I'm saying *if,* not saying he *did*—he probably did it because he *is* a dog. They do some pretty outrageous things, even the best of them. They don't think, for Christ's sake. They aren't in any way the same as we are. They have great noses, and good ears, and great bloody big teeth, but they don't think far enough ahead or symbolically enough to take a leather chair for anything but a leather chair. To a dog, that's what it is. It's not a substitute for a person, or a symbolic warning. They haven't got the smarts for that. To them, it's just a great, big chewable object."

I'm making an ass of myself, thought Peter. But he went ahead anyway. "But could he do it if she told him to?"

Rog's response was a whoop of disbelieving laughter. "Isabelle? Your Isabelle? Oh, I grant you she's got him well trained. But can you seriously imagine her ordering her prize-winning dog to rough up your damned chair, man? Be serious." There was a long pause. "Be serious, Pete," he said again.

But Peter only stood up and stared out his window, counting taxicabs on Park Avenue fourteen floors below. He fingered the change in his pocket, trying, by his silence, to jog Rog into saying something more, something that would put this thing together for him.

"Pete? Are you still there?"

"Yes. I'm still here. Sure," he answered, his voice uninflected.

Rog hesitated, and then went on. "Look, Pete. Do you want to hear the only odd story I've ever heard about Beau? Okay, I'll tell you. Evvy told me that Beau went home as early as he did because he *wanted* to—that Izzy went to visit, and that after she left he howled until she came back and got him. Now, I can't believe that, and I'm sure you can't. Sheerest coincidence, right?"

"I'd say so, Rog. Except that Isabelle never told me that story at all, and we had quite a discussion about bringing him home so young. Otherwise I'd think so, maybe. But I don't."

He heard Rog slam his hand down on his desk. "God damn it, Pete. This is the real world. You're nervous because he tore up a kid who damned well deserved tearing up—tore him up out of that great instinct a dog has for his own turf and his own people. This is ridiculous."

Peter nodded. "That's the instinct I guess I'm talking about. Maybe he thinks I'm on his turf, and maybe he thinks I'm infringing on Isabelle's attention. Who can tell? Ever since we got him, we've had more than our share of disagreements—some kind of real anger working, something. I don't know."

"Pete, get your mind on something else. You're jealous of a dog, for Christ's sake, and you've tried to talk her into getting rid of it. That's why she didn't tell you about the chair, probably. He's not even aggressive. He's never bitten anyone but a guy who had a gun on Izzy. He's under her control, perfectly well behaved, with a shelf full of trophies to prove it." Suddenly Rog's voice turned hard and sharp. "If this is some number to enlist me in getting rid of Beau for you, I'm not going to play. That's final."

"No, no. It isn't that, Rog. You know me better than that."

"Well, you've asked me before, you know. Look, I'm just telling you to ease up. Who knows dogs better than I do? Come on, it's all right," said Rog.

Peter laughed at the perfect conviction in his voice. Of course he was right. He had to be right. "Okay, Rog. I guess I'm just jumpy, but you've certainly got logic on your side. So let me make it up to you, and come to dinner tomorrow night. Isabelle would love to see you, too. And I'm sorry as hell. Six o'clock good for you?"

"Couldn't be better. I'm going to have a hell of an afternoon, taking O'Toole up to see some Gordon setters in Pound Ridge. And don't worry about this. You've got to promise me."

"Sure, Rog, sure. See you then."

After Peter had hung up the phone, he leaned back in his chair, closed his eyes for a moment, and felt the tension slide out of him. It was all right, had to be all right. Something like the burglary would be enough to set anyone's imagination working overtime. He sat up and dialed his home number, to let Isabelle know that Rog would be coming to dinner tomorrow. And then he'd get down to business.

Friday night found Rog at the Hutchinsons', stretched out on the sofa, idly contemplating a hole in one sock as he sipped the last of some after-dinner Grand Marnier. Tom, with a wink, refilled his glass. "So, what are you thinking about, Rog? It's not like you to be meditative."

Rog snorted, and propped himself a little higher on his elbow. "Oh, Christ. I talked with Pete Buckingham this morning, and he was all in a snit. Losing his grip or working too hard or something," he said.

"He must have been upset by the burglary," Evvy chimed in. "If it hadn't been for Beau, God alone knows what might have happened."

Rog shook his head. "What's got him going isn't that, though I guess it has to do with that. Something about the dog tearing up his chair. And something about that story you told me about his going home early. Izzy didn't tell him about that."

"What about his chair?" said Tom.

"He's sure the dog tore up his chair, just before Izzy had the new upholstery put on," said Rog. "Anyway, he's got himself about three-quarters convinced that the animal is dangerous, and I think he has the idea that Izzy tells him to do things like that. I don't know. He seems to be driving at something that doesn't make much sense to me."

"Makes sense to me," Evvy volunteered. "I've watched her work with Beau, and she's told me stories about him. It certainly could be. I bred him, and I have these two dogs, but I've never seen the kind of connection before that I see with Isabelle and Beau."

"Like what?" said Rog, sitting up.

"Well, like that thing about the hurdle—the one that Pete built. He'd no more than finished it when Beau went and jumped it both ways. No instruction, nothing. Just jumped it," said Evvy. "That was weird. And the thing about his going home. Laugh if you want, but I *know* what happened."

Tom laughed. "Fascinating, darling. Tell us more."

She failed to catch his joking tone, and frowned, thinking hard. "The real thing is that she's had such an easy time training him. I mean, we've done it quite a lot, and with his parent stock. And we work at it, believe me. But she hasn't had to at all." She turned to her husband. "Don't you think, Tom?"

"I've never thought about it, but I guess you're right. In all the time we've been in the game, I can't think of any dog that went so far so young, especially under an inexperienced trainer. No way," he answered.

"But, honey, doesn't that seem odd to you? And Rog, what do you think?"

Rog, for the moment, said nothing, but Tom poured himself some more Grand Marnier and leaned back in his chair. "I just haven't thought about it. Been too busy contemplating the return of the next litter, I have to admit. But now that I think of it, I guess it seems a little strange—not exactly threatening, but strange."

Rog contemplated the ceiling, pure exasperation on his face. "So bloody what, you two? What is this all supposed to add up to?" he said.

Tom leaned forward, elbows on knees. "Look, Rog. There's some degree of communication between any owner and any animal, and the more they're together—and the more sensitive they are—the greater it is. Dogs respond to all kinds of things—scent, mood, tone of voice, and so forth. If one of the kids has hurt feelings, Serena and Brum will pile into his room and make a big deal of him until they've got him cheered up. And if there's a fight, they'll get upset. Things like that. But training isn't usually like that. For it to be really *easy*, there'd just about have to be some degree not just of intelligence on the part of the dog, but of communication on some other level. That's a guess, but Beau and Isabelle are together a lot, and he may be just awfully sensitive to her moods—like when she was scared the other night. Things like that. He could be just as sensitive to what she wants him to do, but that's a big jump, I know."

Rog's patience with this was wearing thin. "That's nonsense, don't you think? To make a jump like that? I usually have a half-dozen dogs around, and none of them have done that."

"But none of them were pups when you got them, and, besides, they're in a pack, not a one-to-one situation," said Tom.

"This is all just silly," said Evvy. "What does it matter, as long as none of us has crossed Beau lately?"

Tom swirled the brown liquid in his glass for a long moment. "I guess it doesn't," he said.

Roger's enthusiasm for Ellen O'Toole was slim enough, made slimmer by a Grand Marnier hangover that made his head ache and his stomach miserable. Standing at his kitchen counter, ladling dog food into bowls as his animals skulked around his feet, he couldn't contemplate his plan to pick her up at ten. He'd have to call her, and postpone until one-thirty. It would have to be at least that late, or he'd be stuck with taking her to lunch. And that was the last damned thing he could think of right now, absolutely the last.

He looked up her number and called her. Even though she'd dropped her hectoring manner at his show of interest and attention, even though she was behaving almost coyly, her voice was like a chain saw. But she was agreeable. Yes, one-thirty would be fine. He'd have time to go to the Y, swim and have a shower, and have a sandwich and a bloody mary somewhere before he picked her up. All that talk about dogs last night. You'd think he'd have had the sense to ask for some coffee.

By the time he picked her up, he felt better, his old jovial self, despite weather that seemed to be all the bad things November could bring—gray, cold, bleak, and bare, with the threat of snow or sleet on the wind. Madeleine had died in November, in weather like this. It made him hurt to think of it, made him feel old. At least he'd be busy today, busy enough to drive it out of his mind for a while. He handed Miss O'Toole a blanket, since the heater wasn't adequate, and turned north, through New Canaan to Pound Ridge. It was surprising how easy it was to keep up a conversation with this woman, surprising how amiable she seemed, and how talkative. All he had to do was nod every once in a while.

It seemed that she'd grown up in Darien, gone to Bryn Mawr, taught for years in a private school around Philadelphia. When her parents had died, she'd given up her teaching, purchased the cottage, and settled down to live on her pension and the small amount of interest. Not a bad life, as she said. But perhaps she should have done it in the area where she'd lived for so long.

Not that she'd ever had all that many friends. She'd had her dogs over the years—all cairns, all named Toto, from *The Wizard of Oz*. Perhaps too lively for a woman her age, though, but scrappy fellows, just as good as any big dog at keeping a criminal at bay.

"Do you know the Buckinghams?" Rog

asked. "They live right down the road from you, and their Belgian just kept one at bay—in spades. Did you know about it?" He was ready to tell the whole story, but Ellen O'Toole sniffed, a sound of high disdain.

"Well, I wouldn't be surprised at anything that dog did. Vicious, that one. Almost attacked Toto and me that day at Ox Ridge, he did. And, of course, you know that Mrs. Buckingham cheats like mad. I filed a complaint about that after the Ox Ridge show, believe me."

Rog held back a smile. The complaint had been thrown out.

"I knew you'd filed a complaint, but I've known Isabelle Buckingham for years, and I'm sure she didn't cheat. And I've known Beau since he was whelped, and I really don't think you can say he's vicious. He's devoted to Isabelle, but he'd never hurt anyone who didn't actually threaten her. That young man had a gun on her, you know."

"Dr. Stanley," she said primly, shifting in her seat, "it has to be cheating. You'd better believe I told her so, too, that day at the show. Shocking, but I'm the sort of woman who speaks her mind, as you can certainly tell. You should have seen that dog of hers—growling at Toto and me like some kind of wild animal, crouched and ready to spring on us. Shocking! I'm glad he caught that burglar, but you mark my words: that's a bad, bad dog."

Roger thought back to the tiny, dead cairn

lying on the autopsy table, the neck snapped but the body unmarked. He hadn't been able to tell how it happened, but it had happened. He tried to add it together. Beau's going home. The hurdle. Peter's chair. The burglar. He flexed his shoulders, thinking as she prattled on.

Whatever this woman was talking about, however badly she misperceived it, she was saying, in essence, what Peter and Evvy and Tom had already tried to tell him. That something odd was going on with Isabelle and Beau, something beyond training and command. Something in some new territory that was beyond his understanding.

She jogged his elbow. "Is anything the matter, Dr. Stanley? You look rather odd. Is anything the matter?" she was saying.

"No, I'm sorry. Just wool-gathering." He managed a smile. "I'm not used to company. I generally drive by myself—bachelor habit, since my wife died."

And soon she was chattering again, apologizing for perhaps saying something out of line about a woman who was, after all, his friend. Then they'd arrived at the breeder's and were surrounded by a tangle of black and tan dogs and puppies. Within an hour he'd helped her settle on a chubby, stolid little bitch whose smooth temperament was obviously a good foil for someone as fretful and nervous as Miss O'Toole. She was pleased, and so was Roger.

On the way back home, he let her talk, and she bubbled over with enthusiasm for her new pup, her gratitude for his help. He tried to nod and make the appropriate noises, tried to think as he drove, but his sense of unease came back. He shoved it aside by taking a more active part in the conversation—the requirements of puppies, appropriate names, anything that came into his head and suited the occasion. He heaved a sigh of relief when he dropped her off. It was four-thirty, and he was due at the Buckinghams' at six. He'd shower and shave and feed the animals and try to puzzle the thing out. Try to make it add up to something other than what it seemed to be.

15

In the Buckinghams' kitchen, Peter was checking the supply of liquor and mix, emptying trays of ice into the ice bucket, setting out glasses, while Isabelle stood at the sink, snipping delicately at a potted tarragon plant whose leaves would go to flavor the salad dressing. "Let's see," she was saying.

"We've got the shrimp salad, and the veal Cordon Bleu, and pineapple for dessert. I guess we'll need a white wine, something with some body to it. What would you think?"

Peter, still smarting over a tennis match lost that morning to Charlie MacDougall, snapped at her in annoyance. "No, Isabelle. Red to stand up against the veal and ham combination with the Mornay sauce. Better a red—Médoc or Graves or something."

"If you say so," she said mildly, "but I still think of white with veal."

"An inadequate generalization, really, Isabelle. I ought to know, for God's sake, after all these years of keeping book on it. You'd think that some of it would rub off by now." That sounded harsh, and he knew it. He softened his tone. "Look, I'm due in France right after the first of the year. Come with me, and we'll do a real tour. I'll teach you everything I know about it—demonstrations and the works. Change your mind and come."

She turned to him in surprise. "Peter, we've been through this before. I told you, I don't want to go. I'd like it if we'd have a real vacation—take Beau with us and go off to Vermont for a few days, something like that. But I don't want to sit somewhere, waiting for you to finish working. Can't you understand that?"

He glanced across the kitchen, where Beau, now on the alert, had been stretched out under the table. "Well, here we are back at Beau again," he said. "I know I talked you into that dog, but I'm just a little tired of Beau this and Beau that, not to mention Beau sleeping in the goddamn bed. I know he's something of a star, but I'm damned if I don't also know that he's something of a pain. If I'm permitted to say that without having someone bite my ass off."

She turned back to the sink. "Oh, don't be ridiculous, Peter. He bit one burglar, which is just what he should have done. Now let's get off it and have a nice evening. I've really gone to a lot of trouble with this, and I'd be grateful if you wouldn't spoil it."

He could have left it alone, but he sensed that if he could push her a little farther, he'd have the proof he was looking for. He let a long, silent few seconds pass before he said, with feigned indifference, "Okay. One burglar. And I'd guess one chair."

She wheeled around to face him again, flushing angrily. "I don't know what's the matter with you tonight. My God! What chair? Why do I have to put up with this?" Beau had scrambled to his feet and was suddenly by her side, glancing anxiously from her to Peter and back again.

"My chair," he shot at her. "The torn sleeve of Russo's jacket and the torn leather from my chair looked just alike. I think Beau tore them both, and that you covered for him; and I don't know why. I heard a story about why he came home so early—and I didn't hear it from you. I got it from Rog, who got it from Evvy. And I don't know why. I'm saying that I don't like the way he acts, and I'm not just all that crazy about the way you're acting either. I want to get to the bottom of it, and I want to get rid of the dog."

But Isabelle didn't rise to that, barely raised her voice, though her words were harsh. "Peter, you are simply a much bigger fool than I thought you were. We are not getting rid of Beau. You have no idea how fortunate you are that I've had nothing more than a dog in that bed, this last year or two. I wouldn't want to think what or who you've had in yours. And I don't know what this is supposed to be about chairs, but I'm going to take a shower and change and try to enjoy a pleasant evening with an old friend. This is a pointless discussion, and I'm not going on with it." She wiped her hands on a dishtowel, and bent to pat Beau.

"Don't let him upset you, old fellow. Not ever," she said. She turned abruptly and left the room, leaving Peter to stare after her. Beau, for once, did not follow her, but sat where he had been left, looking amiably, almost playfully, at Peter.

"Maybe what you need, Beau, is just a firm talking to," he said, "and not all this fussing. You're really a pretty good dog. Yes, a good dog." He held his hand out, and Beau came over, sniffed it, and gave it a tentative lick. Peter scratched his ears, and the big dog leaned against his leg in obvious pleasure.

"You just need a firm hand, don't you, dog, hmmm?" he said, crouching down to put his head at the same level as Beau's. "All that training, and all those trophies—well, they're nice enough, but not as good as being just a good family pet. Right?" The dog laid his head against Peter's arm, just as Patch had always done, offering his neck for scratching. After all the months of snubs, all the fighting, it was a relief to see him acting like what he should be, and for a long moment, Peter responded to it, rubbing the dog's neck, stroking him gently, pleased. Finally he stood up.

"Well, I guess that's it, Beau, and we can be friends from now on. But we'll have to take it up later, because I've got to go get the wine. Okay?" He started out to the living room, and Beau came with him, tagging at his heels as he had so often tagged at Isabelle's. He even accompanied him down the steep, narrow stairs to the cellar and followed him as he checked the labels on the bottles. Finally Peter selected a Chablis to have with the salad and a fine red Médoc for the main course. He moved the Médoc with extraordinary gentleness, placing it in the crook of his arm in exactly the same position it had occupied on the rack. As he turned with the wines, he caught Beau's eye. "Not for dogs, of course, but a great pleasure for people, Beau."

Beau seemed delighted with the attention. He was nearly dancing with it, frisking around Peter's feet. *Such a responsive animal,*

Peter thought, *now that he knows what's what and who's who. Really not a bad dog at all.* But as he started toward the stairs, Beau at his heels, the dog tangled in his feet. "Hey! Watch it! You'll trip me up," he cried. Beau stopped immediately. "Come on," Peter said. "I'll go upstairs and decant this, and then I'll take you out for a run. Okay?"

But Beau was at it again, wilder than ever, romping as Peter had seen him romp with Isabelle outdoors. Now Beau was blocking him from the stairs, nipping at his feet, whirling around him so rapidly that he could barely move. "Stop it, Beau! No!" he yelled. But it was no use.

He tried calling Isabelle, but he could hear the water still cascading down the pipes from the shower. He knew she could not hear him. Slowly and carefully, he edged toward the stairs, still cradling the Médoc in one arm, and holding the Chablis in his free hand. At last, Beau made way for him, and he was perhaps halfway up the stairs when the animal brushed by him and then moved around to face him.

In an awful parody of affection, a grim caricature of play, and with an expression of the utmost eagerness on his face, Beau launched himself at Peter and knocked him backward down the stairs.

It seemed to take a long time, and Peter's eyes and mind took in everything—the dog coming at him, the weight against his chest, his feet going out from under him, his arms stupidly tightening their hold on the wine. He noticed that there were cobwebs in the angle of the stairs, had time to notice that, just before his head struck the floor at an angle and with a force that simultaneously fractured his skull and snapped his neck.

Mercifully, he felt almost nothing, and, in that last instant, all he could feel was a certain satisfaction, knowing he'd been right all along about Beau. As he lay silent, the Chablis bottle, cracked, leaked its contents onto the floor. But the Médoc rested secure and unbroken on his chest.

Beau sniffed around him, and then padded quietly up the stairs to the second floor. He lay down outside the bathroom door, put his head on his paws, and fell asleep.

16

There was talk, of course. It began right after the funeral, which Isabelle had attended on John's arm, with Beau at her side. It gained impetus from the flat refusal of either Rog Stanley or the Hutchinsons to comment on it one way or the other, and took wing when it became clear enough that they'd stopped seeing Isabelle.

Ellen O'Toole was behind a good deal of it, and though she was, at the best of it, neither pleasant nor well-liked, a good many people listened to her long enough to think that, whatever the truth was, it might be prudent to avoid Isabelle and Beau.

As for Isabelle, she seemed unbothered. She remained in the house, dealt intelligently with the attorneys and accountants on whom her future now depended, and kept to her daily rounds with Beau always at her side. She still walked on the beach in fine weather, and she redecorated the study. Her only guest was Amos Roberts, who seemed as devoted to her as ever.

In that harshest of winters, she lent him Peter's Porsche, which he drove as slowly as if it were a Model T. He had lunch or supper with her at least twice a week. He changed the storm windows and doors for her the week after Peter's funeral, helped her to rake and bag the leaves, and helped her to shovel her walks and driveway.

In February, he accompanied her and Beau to Westminster, where Beau went best of breed and finished his championship. In March, he helped her plant a vegetable garden. People thought it was an odd friendship, and said so. Zizi Roberts pronounced herself too embarrassed by the whole thing even to talk about it. And so the months went by.

Night after night, during that long winter, Roger Stanley would sit by his fire, his own animals around him, and go over it again and again. The shock of that November evening had been considerable, and there'd been a lot of talk, but the more he thought about it, the more he had to believe that Peter's fall had been a coincidence, had to be, could be nothing else. The evidence to the contrary was too flimsy, too much a product of odd theories, speculations, circumstances. Beau might have torn up a chair, had torn up a burglar. He could have killed the cairn. But that didn't necessarily mean that he, or Isabelle, had had anything to do with Peter's death. It was chance, after all, that the fall had killed him. Besides, not even Ellen O'Toole had accused Beau of any further misdeeds.

And what was his part in this? That he'd believed those stories for a while? Half-believed them, anyway. No, the worst of it was that he'd avoided Isabelle all winter, been rude to the widow of one of his oldest friends. It was cruelty, plain and simple, and enough time had gone by that he was ashamed—too ashamed to call her, or ask her out, or casually drop by. He would do it soon, he promised himself. But he didn't.

Finally, it was spring, and late on a particular April afternoon, when the trees were leafing out and the daffodils and tulips were briefly in bloom at the same time, he found himself running early to a cocktail party at one of the new houses on the very tip of the Neck. On the most sudden of impulses, he checked his watch and hit the brakes a few yards short of Isabelle's driveway, turning rapidly, skidding on the gravel.

He felt awkward as he climbed out of the car and walked to the front door. It had been so long since he'd been there, and he didn't know what to say or how to begin to say it. He rang the bell and stood with his head bent, waiting for the sound of Isabelle's footsteps, trying desperately to think how to get through those first few minutes. But what he heard was a long, low growl, deep and threatening, and then the soothing sound of Isabelle's voice. Finally, she called through the door, "Is that Roger?"

"Yes, Izzy. May I come in?"

"Of course, you silly thing. Just a minute." And then she threw the door open and beamed at him. She looked marvelous, better than she had in years. "I'm sorry Beau growled," she said. "We haven't had many visitors lately, and he's not accustomed to company."

She swung the screen door open, and stood aside to let him enter, turning to Beau to say, "Look, give him a sniff. It's just Rog, and not a stranger at all."

This Beau did, and then followed them into the kitchen while Isabelle fixed Roger and herself a drink. "You must see the study, Rog. I've had it redone since you were here last. Come on," she said, handing him his drink and leading the way. She waved him into Peter's old chair, Beau between them, and nodded with pleasure at his compliments.

At last, she settled back in her chair and leveled a steady gaze at him. "Well, really, Rog. Tell me what brings you down here after all these months. Friendship? Or curiosity about the witch and her familiar?" Her smile was tight, her voice edged with sarcasm.

"That's not fair, Izzy. I'm sorry I haven't come. Ashamed, even. Maybe I shouldn't have after all."

"I didn't say that, Rog. This should have been an ordeal, but it doesn't bother me that much. I was surprised at you and the Hutchinsons, but I can understand it. Being a widow isn't exactly new to me, either, you know. For years I turned into a sort of widow on Monday and stayed a widow through Thursday. And I put up with Peter's sleeping around, as you must know. For years, it was anyone but me. So it's not so hard, not really." She paused, and sipped her drink.

"I'm sure people think it's strange that we're so friendly with Captain Roberts, but we like him and he likes us. And we can do things for one another. I know he's a little strange, but so what?"

Roger had been prepared for anything but frankness, and it caught him unawares. He made a grab at putting the conversation on a more conventional track. "Isabelle," he said formally, "I'm really glad to know that things are going so well. I know how hard it is. I've been through it. And I think you're adjusting so beautifully."

She stopped him with a burst of laughter. "Adjusted? Oh, Rog, you just have to be kidding. The whole town has gone around for months gossiping that my dog killed my husband, probably at my instigation, certainly with my approval. So don't you think it's just a little peculiar to talk about adjusting, for God's sake?"

He tried again, in a slightly different direction. "Isabelle, dearest Izzy," he said, leaning forward earnestly. "I know there's been talk of that kind, and I know that it's nasty and vicious and untrue and crazy. I mean, Peter was upset about Beau, and even kind of jealous..." It occurred to him that it wasn't a good idea to get into that, so he let the thought die out, and swirled the ice in his glass.

"Is it untrue, Rog? Is it crazy? I know what Peter told you. It's true about the chair. It's true about why Beau came home. He wanted to come home." She leaned back and smiled.

"And that O'Toole woman's dog? I don't know. It could be. If so, it was the best thing that could have happened to that poor dog. And Peter? Well, we had an argument that night. Peter wanted to get rid of Beau, and we argued about it, and then I went upstairs to take a shower. I don't know what happened after that, but it could be." She thought for a long moment, not looking at Rog, not seeing the expression on his face.

"Beau's my best friend, you know. He'd do anything for me, Rog. Anything at all, I think," she said.

Roger finished his drink, and set his glass down. He stood, forcing a smile, but keeping a wary eye on Beau.

"I must be off, dear girl," he said, a shade too heartily. "But the next time I won't be so long, I promise. No wonder this whole thing has upset you so, and I wish there was some way I could apologize for my part in it. I truly am sorry."

She and Beau walked with him to the door. Only as he was leaving did she touch him lightly on the arm and say, "Don't apologize. I've got a good life, you know. And I'll be glad to see you any time, but only if you can come out of friendship, and not out of guilt."

He knew that he could not, but he took her hand in his, and said, "I will. And soon." As he pulled out of the driveway, he could see her in the fading light, waving him off, with Beau standing faithfully by her side.

If you have your heart set on Romance, read

Coventry Romances

Each Coventry Romance is a love story rich in the customs and manners of England during the Regency, Georgian, Victorian, or Edwardian periods.

Beginning in November, there will be six new novels every month by such favorite authors as Sylvia Thorpe, Claudette Williams, and Rebecca Danton who will make you feel the elegance and grandeur of another time and place.

Look for the Coventry Romance displays wherever paperbacks are sold.

*Let Coventry give you
a little old-fashioned romance.*